I0747456

THE TRAVELLER

LIN BETANCOURT

Cover design by Judith S. Design & Creativity
www.judithsdesign.com
Published by Glass Spider Publishing
www.glassspiderpublishing.com

Also by Lin Betancourt

The Grandfather Trilogy (composed of)
Grandfathers and Demons
The Dybbuk Did It
Genghis Cat and His Children

The Alligator and the Astronaut

Life and Afterlife

With Nia Lichtenstein and R Henry Price:
Cat Mountain

This book is dedicated to…

Lorna, for her encouragement and ideas—

Richard, for his help and criticism—

And the mice, but that is not an invitation to return.
You know what you did.

Part One: Sonia
Pre-pandemic

Chapter One

By opening her eyes and listening and tasting she had earned
her own fortune –Max Apple, *The Propheteers*

I work, but I think about Norway during the night. I think
Norway is as shining clean as this hospital. Green trees
and fresh snow everywhere. And during the night, it is
quiet here, the way I imagine Norway to be…except there,
surely, you can hear the wind in the trees.

I work sixteen-hour shifts at this hospital. I need the
money. They don't pay much here, making an exception for
doctors, of course. This is a university town. We have a re-
newable population of nurses…their husbands graduate from
the master and doctoral programs, and they move on, and are
replaced by others. I earn more at the Center in the next town,
but I only work there on weekends.

Joanne calls me to help her turn the woman in 334 over.
She's old and disoriented and she has a strong Irish accent.
When I go in the room, she pats Joanne's belly and says, "I

used to be flat like you." Joanne says "Ugh!" and starts laughing. Joanne is pretty and blond, no one cares that she comes in late and never does her charts on time. I am plain brown, eyes, hair, and personality. I have to do everything perfectly right, just to keep my job.

It doesn't matter because I am a traveller. Almost no one knows this about me. In a hospital, seeing is distorted. People are practically stone blind. All they see is a woman dressed in scrubs. Ah, I am not a man, so I must be a nurse. Nurse, can you help me? Nurse, can you come to my room? Nurse, my aunt's been ringing her bell for twenty minutes!

You put a label on people, and right away, they use it as an excuse not to see you. It's not just nurses, it happens to doctors and police officers, too.

It's terrible not to see people as they really are. My scrubs contribute to my invisibility and sometimes, when I leave the hospital, I don't want to take them off. So, people don't see me when I am shopping or waiting for the bus, either. They say things in front of me that they would never say to anyone else.

Very few know how to see. One I meet right in this hospital. I am working my way around my rooms at four o'clock in the morning. I have my flashlight to check that people are still breathing, my thermometer to take their temperatures, and my sphygmomanometer to measure their blood pressure. My pockets are stuffed full of thermometer covers to keep germs from spreading, and little pieces of paper to record my notes. I look like a kangaroo wearing scrubs.

This man is awake. To be honest, I almost don't see him.

I am trained to be blind, too. I should see someone who is awake when he is supposed to be asleep. I should whisper, "You're supposed to be asleep!" and walk away.

But this man has shiny eyes. He thanks me for taking his temperature and asks if I have a minute to talk. I remember what it's like to feel connected with someone…like beads strung on a necklace, gently touching each other's sides.

His roommate is a college kid who is sucking his thumb and breathing through his adenoids. We talk quietly so as not to wake him.

We talk about the night…the quiet time, the feeling of power you get from being up when the rest are asleep. "Night becomes you," he says.

"That's because the night is made for travellers."

"Where are you going next?"

"Norway," I answer.

He smiles. "I wish you could take me with you."

I want to tell him that everyone is a traveller in some sense of the word. When you are completely still—when you cease to travel—you are dead. But I know better than to say that to a patient. I smile and turn away.

I never see him again. He travels on to his own destination.

Some people think that travelling is a lost art. For me, there is nothing like the excitement of being between two places. It doesn't matter where you are—even if you're stuck in traffic, it's good, so good not to be home. If I could, I would travel all the time.

The way I live my life, material possessions don't tie me down. That would make it hard for me to travel. I live in a little apartment in this town. Except for my cat and my fossils, I don't own anything I value.

I am lucky to have a photographic memory. After I read all the details of the place I am to travel to, I can throw the packet away. Now the place is mine forever.

I feel that way about attachments, too. It is better not to have them. It might make it hard to leave. Of course I have some. I am married, and I have a child. Leaving Peter and Sara is hard, but I believe I'm stronger for it.

You may want to know why I left my family. Have you read the book *Metamorphosis* by Franz Kafka? One day, Gregor Samsa wakes up and finds he has become a giant insect. This is what happens to me. No, not physically, but this is how I feel. No one can see that I am an insect. I know that Peter and Sara thought I was normal. In some ways, that makes it worse, I think, than it was for Gregor.

Gregor dies in the book, but I get to leave. For both of us, it is better not to be around your family when you feel this way.

I carry Sara in my head, along with all the beautiful places where I travel. And I don't think about Peter often. Not too often.

This is how I learn to travel. When I graduate from high school, some people I know are going to Europe, and I want to go too. They aren't my friends, but they are in my classes, and I can share expenses for the trip with the money people give me when I graduate.

My parents don't understand. They make up a lot of excuses to explain why I can't go. It costs too much. They are afraid I will get hurt. Blah blah blah.

I will settle for a lot less than Europe—even a train ride to Canada. But nothing? That is too little, even for me. I feel like somebody ranking high in the universe is against me. I imagine an old lady dressed in a black cape and top hat, snickering "Aha!" as she watches me never get what I want—never.

So that is the first time I travel. I can't go to Europe with my friends, so I go to the library and read. I concentrate on Paris. I read every book they have. If anyone asks me, I can talk about my trip to Paris for hours.

But no one asks me.

I am accepted at a small liberal arts college in Pennsylvania, where I get my nursing degree. I am supposed to be a registered nurse because that's like being a secretary—you can always walk into a hospital and get a job if you're an RN with experience.

That summer before I leave for college, I work in the library, shelving the books that other people take out. Do you know that most people write incredibly badly, yet they get published for writing formulaic shit that appeals to the masses? I look at the books as I put them away, and maybe one in one hundred is worth reading.

Well, maybe more of them are worth reading in the travel section.

In that section, I read about England. That's a good place to travel. There is a museum in Oxford called the Ashmolean. It has watercolors by Max Beerbohm tucked away in the back. If you ask the curator, he will let you look at them, but you have to wear a pair of white gloves, and you have to sign in and out of a great ledger.

Max Beerbohm leaves those pictures to the Ashmolean because he loves Oxford. Sometimes I wish for something to leave to someone, too. I would like someone to remember me, even if they only read a little plaque about me in front of a glass museum case.

As a young adult, I want to earn that plaque. Someday, I will become a great traveller.

Except now I know better.

Now I know that it is not important for other people to notice you.

Now I know it's better to stay alone in your head.

It's like my mother says— "The only things you can rely on in this world are books." Well, I am young and foolish, and I think that is a terrible thing to say to a child, but now I know she is right—except, for me, it's travelling, instead of books. The books are a means to an end, like working in the hospital to support myself.

Before I discover my gift for travelling, my brother is better at everything we do. It is a terrible feeling because I knew my parents prefer him to me. I understand why, because he really is so much smarter and handsomer and more talented than I am.

We both have the same music lessons, but he is the one who is the prodigy. All I can do is try to get my fingers to move fast enough so my father doesn't slap me and make me wet my pants.

I never hear music in my head the way my brother does.

I am never good at math.

These are my faults.

Oh, and I am never good at chess.

I think, now, it is because I know the chess pieces will never get off the board— they are doomed to travel from one side to another.

I like it when my brother captures all my pieces, because at least they get off the terrible preassigned squares. I want the knights to be horses, and I want them to run far away from home.

As far away as Norway.

Chapter Two

Ah, God damn fear and damn my self that fears
To fling my love like rice across your face
—unpublished poet

Tonight, I travel to Fatepur Sikri, the city created entirely of red sandstone. It looks like a city of blood. Emperor Akbar means it to be his capital when he builds it in 1569—perhaps that year blood is on his mind. He deserts it sixteen years later.

Men are like that—they build cities, get married—in Akbar's case this happens more than once—and then something comes up and they ride away, never to return. But if they come back, they expect women to be waiting for them, as if we turn to stone the moment they disappear.

I meet Peter, who becomes my husband, by the ocean, on an August day. I have an unusual job in Nantucket. I work for two doctors who ask me to take care of their children so they can take a month's vacation. They go out to restaurants every night and to the beach every day. They pay me a good salary plus all my expenses, and in return, for a month, I get to play in the ocean with two little boys and a little girl. It doesn't seem like work, but they pay me anyway.

The sun bleaches my hair blond, and my skin light brown. I look like Nordic furniture. I think that's what makes Peter notice me, because usually I am invisible. I see him watching me while I play with the children in the ocean. He is small and clean and dressed like the earth, in green.

He doesn't speak to me right away. Instead, he goes over to the sandy oasis where my employers the doctors are sunbathing and drinking and talks to them first.

"Who is that guy talking to Mommy?" Brian asks. He is the oldest of the children, and the one who is most aware of the differences between children and adults. Usually, he doesn't think the differences are good ones.

It turns out Peter is a friend—or what passes for a friend, someone who shares some of your experiences and geographic background for an influential period of your life.

In this case, Peter and the doctors that I work for know each other from being would-be interns in med school. During that time, they study to be radiologists, the specialty with the most distance from actual patients. It's for intellectuals with good analytic skills. Instead of touching flesh, they look at computer-generated pictures.

This med school experience helps them form some sort of bond that I somehow miss forming with most of the people in my nursing classes. They laugh and talk together; I think that means Peter must be a good guy.

At some point, the doctors call us all over to be introduced. The children are shy, and I am not interested, so Peter sets himself to win us all over to his side.

He is about ten years older, just as the doctors are older, but while I think they are ancient, he seems younger and more relaxed. He brings a recorder to the beach, and plays so the children can dance, but he isn't watching them, he is watching me.

I know Peter is watching me. I am flattered. The children, especially the little girl, know this extra attention is all about me, not them, and they are unusually badly behaved, whining and throwing sand at each other.

Children always know when something is about to change.

"What kind of music do you like?" Peter asks me between songs.

"I don't like music," I say. "In fact, I hate it."

Peter looks surprised. "Really? Why?"

"Because" I say, "my brother is a musician."

That makes Peter even more interested, but I am used to people who only want to know about my brother, and not about me.

Maybe because I won't answer his questions, while we are in Nantucket, he takes me out to dinner on the one night that I have time to myself.

I am nervous because he is so much prettier than I am. I go to the Marimekko store and find a very simple dress that is on sale, but I still think I don't measure up to his looks.

Peter has violet blue eyes and thick brown hair. He is only a little taller than I am, but that doesn't bother me because I never wear heels, they're way too uncomfortable.

Everyone wears bathing suits in Nantucket, but he wears a brown suit to the restaurant. I am afraid the whole meal will take place in silence; in fact, I bring a Rebecca West book with me in case this really happens.

But Peter asks me about the book, and it's easy for me to talk about books.

"What do you like to do when you're not working?" he asks.

"I like wasting my time on unimportant things that don't matter," I say. I am not going to tell him that I am a traveller.

"I don't believe that," Peter says. "I see you taking care of the children. When you play with them, you have every detail planned.

"So, what do you like, Sonia, really?"

Peter waits for me to unravel, but I shake my head and stay silent. I won't be so foolish as to trust him.

"Well, if you're determined to remain a mystery, we'll change the subject. Let me tell you what I like, then," he says easily. "I like to travel."

When he tells me about rowing down the Ganges and all the birds he has seen, I almost cry. But still, I won't talk about myself.

I don't think I will ever see Peter again after we leave Nantucket. But when we get back to Pennsylvania, he shows up at my dorm. The doctors give him all my information, and I think that counts as a reference.

I like talking to Peter, which is deceiving.

Or maybe I don't like talking to him, but I do like listening.

I never have to say much. To start a conversation, I ask Peter about all the places he travels to, and when he answers, I am really interested. I don't have to pretend.

At that age, you don't know what is permanent and what you can change. But it is very dangerous to give yourself permission to fall in love with a man.

What if he can tell within a minute of meeting you that you would rather be with him than alone with yourself?

What if he's more in love with you than you are with him?

I am barely twenty years old, and at that age, having someone pay attention and talk to you means so much. You don't know what you can change about a man, or what will change you.

If you haven't fucked much, that can be confusing as well. It's hard to tell the difference between a man who loves you and a man who only wants to fuck you.

Especially if the man has the kind of hair that should rightly belong to a woman, and the kind of mouth that says brilliant things before it kisses you.

My marriage is a not too small box. I can, with only a little effort, touch the top or bend to the bottom.

The floor of the box is a square. Let us say that of the sides too and call the box a cube.

Now, I can, in this box, dance a little dance. No, not an Isadora Duncan floating dance with scarves, but a dance none the less.

A step to the side, most likely; and that makes me think the box might be bigger on the inside than it looks on the outside.

A tantalizing dance, with proper attention given for the

dimensions of the cube in relation to the dancer.

Yes, I can dance some hours of the day inside my box. For quarters, perhaps, or euros if we are on vacation in France.

It depends upon the music, which comes from outside the box, and of course upon whether the people who are always listening think a step-to-the-side dance is too old-fashioned.

The box is not an entirely uncomfortable place to be. Quite the opposite.

I know some who might be afraid of going outside in the real world but who thrive within the cubed box. They do not mind being imprisoned in one place; they do not miss travelling.

In fact, a very small bird, with clipped wings, pecking at dust, might be extremely happy to live in the box. And perhaps that bird never tells anyone else how it wants to travel.

So let there be no mistake, the box can be a marvelous place to live. Unless you start out as a very small bird and grow into someone else after having a child.

I think about how one of the initiation rites of tantric Buddhism is dancing in a graveyard. Another kind of box.

The dance is performed at night. The yogi holds a skull in one hand and a flaming torch in the other.

Women are not allowed to dance this dance, nor to see it.

I see it. It is when I am with Peter.

Crouched low, bare to the waist, the yogi's body glistens with oil above and below his loincloth. He looks like a Pepsi bottle.

His hair is braided to his head so that end is small and unimportant. What matters is the swollen middle and olive legs writhing and gyrating so fast that you swear he is dancing an inch above the gravestone.

Will the enraged captive underground refrain from lifting up an earth clod for one last cynical look?

The dance changes in tempo—becomes so slow that the yogi appears to hang in the air by his arms and legs, suspended by the night.

Throughout I have been aware of the skull. It rides on the end of the torch, is tossed in the air only to come hurtling into the arms of its lover, is rubbed against the skin and passes through the legs of the dancer.

It seems to be looking at me. I ignore it.

The yogi is no longer a person, only a heap of flesh lying on the gravestone. He does not appear to breathe. The torch has burned out. The skull is resting in his hand.

When he moves, I am not sure if he is the same person. I sat in meditation with him two hours ago, but now I can't recognize him.

I look at my husband. He is not the same person either.

"I want to learn the dance," he says to the yogi, and that's when I know our marriage will never last.

Enough of that. I need to pay attention to my patients. I'll drink some more coffee, no matter how awful it tastes.

I'm at the hospital working a double shift because someone called in sick, and I want the overtime. I walk heavier than usual, hoping that makes me seem more authoritative. To make sure I don't look tired, I scramble into clean scrubs in the bathroom. I have to put the old ones in a special container because of the virus. Whoever does the laundry, I hope they're careful to avoid contamination.

I'd like to change my mask between shifts, but we're waiting for a shipment of new protective masks and gowns to come in. We do have plenty of gloves right now, but I don't know how long that will last. From what I see on the news, hospitals all over the United States are having the same problem finding enough personal protective equipment for their staff.

I don't think my thin paper mask is effective after I've worn it for eight hours, but I don't have a choice.

What if it was easy to change into another life? To stop being a nurse and become a yogi, simply by putting on a dhoti?

Or to change a city of sand into a city of blood?

Would anyone or anything stay the same if they have the choice to be different?

Pandemic Phase One
(March through June 2020)

Chapter Three

What is it that troubles you? Death?
–Schemuel Ha-Nagid

In Baja California, on the Pacific coast, gray whales gather every winter. They come from the depths of silence, far and deep—as far as the Bering Sea.

Besides gray whales, there are dolphins, humpbacks, even blues…but now, with global warming, what will happen to them? Will they slowly disappear so that only videos remain? Will they turn into a myth or a story for me to tell my so far fictional grandchildren?

Or will they be replaced by robots so that we will never miss them…unless someday, something goes wrong with the machinery and they sink to the bottom of the ocean, never to be seen again until the ocean dries up.

What will happen then? Will the fish jump out of the receding sea to find their companions?

Will seabirds hide the skies with their wings and circle the shore like airborne watches? Without fish, will they resort to eating us?

I like to watch birds because they know how to see. They'll come right up next to you, no matter how you look, no matter how much money you make, as long as you have the sense to keep still and not frighten them.

The birds remind me of Gulie. I work with Gulie and the other children at the Developmental Center for Children on weekends.

Yeah, I find I need to be around children. Don't make a big deal of it.

Gulie looks exactly like a sketch of a girl…she's so pretty she's not real. She has short red hair, pointed ears, green eyes, and freckles, and she's always in motion. She dances and she runs.

That's the trouble…Gulie can't stop. She has an IQ of fifty, and when you see her from far away, she is perfect. But you can't hold her, because she tears at her hair, and screeches, just like a bird. She rocks back and forth and slaps the side of her head with her hand, then smiles at you from one side of her mouth and dances away, sideways, because she is flat and has no insides.

I remember when I first saw Gulie and the others. I haven't been in this neighborhood very long. This is where I move when I leave Sara and Peter.

I already have a job at the hospital, but I also want to work with children. Getting a part-time job at the Center means a lot to me. It's a government job that pays well.

I pass a test to see if I can give out the complicated

medications these children need. I am proud that I am the only one in the group of nurses to pass the test the first time I take it.

I know I'll be working with children with multiple disabilities, but I don't care. All those silent children, the ones who never talk to anyone. I think they will know right away that I am one of them and they will respond.

I'm good at passing tests, but—you'll laugh. It may seem ridiculous for a traveller, but I get lost a lot.

Absolutely by far the worst part of coming to the Center is following the directions they give me over the phone. I have to leave early because I know I will get lost. I always get lost, sometimes hopelessly lost.

I stop at a gas station and ask for more directions. The men there are careful. They speak to me slowly and I write everything down and tape it to my dashboard. Maybe they think I am damaged, like the children at the Center.

I get here early, after all, and then I have to sit in my car and wait until it is time for my appointment.

The walls of the Center are painted bright colors, and the furniture has clean round lines and no angles. When I come into the main room, I feel like a princess in a fairy tale. I, the royal visitor, almost curtsy to this room full of children.

There are children sitting at desks playing with puzzles; children in corners working with aides; children listening to music and looking out of the window.

Only when I get close do I see that the chairs are wheelchairs and many of the children's heads are being held up by the aides.

Most of the children are drooling, and some are slowly falling sideways out of their chairs. One is having seizures on the carpet, and no one even bothers to look. I am furious.

I would walk away except I know that I belong there.

Now I've been working at the Center for several months, and I hardly see that there's anything different about the children. Some of them even know me or at least they smile when they see me coming with the medications.

Some of them haven't changed at all. Gulie has grown a little taller, but she is microcephalic, born with a very small head, so she does not look much different from the day I met her.

For her birthday, I buy Gulie some new clothes. I shop in the girls' department at Sears, because they have bright primary colors that make Gulie look more than ever like the girl in the Healthtex ad…at least, from far away.

But shopping makes my stomach hurt, because I know I don't really belong there, without a child of my own.

Today, when I come in Gulie runs up to me, puts her head on one side and screams.

"Hi, Gulie!" I say, and bend to hug her, but she doesn't like to be held. She runs away to her corner, and sits slapping the side of her head, smiling and screaming every two minutes.

She is not wearing a mask; it's impossible to keep a mask on her face, and it's like that for almost all the children. Only the nurses and the doctors and the aides wear masks. It makes us look as if we want to rob the children.

Mostly I work during the day here because night at the

Center is terrifying. It's bad enough to work at the hospital where everyone's lives are distorted from fear of a sudden and unexpectedly bad diagnosis. The Center is much worse because many of the children are afraid of the dark. And then, when I hear them crying, so am I.

Jeff is another child with nothing inside. He is like a stuffed animal…a perfect fat little boy, but he hurts me without meaning to, because he is so strong. Sometimes, if I put him to bed when he wants to stay up, he cries, just like a real baby. I have to remind myself that he's more like a hologram than a child.

Because he is so strong, and fights so hard, sometimes I almost lose my patience. I don't though, because if my mood ever becomes dark, Jeff knows how I feel. When he cries, huge tears gush from the round holes that are his eyes. And then I have to comfort him.

Jeff laughs and shouts when he sees me coming, but Louise turns away. She can't even sit up straight in her wheelchair, but she watches me from the corners of her eyes.

Louise hates taking her medication. She is sly and lets it dribble out of her mouth, pretending she can't help it. I just mix it with applesauce and put it back in again. I'm in no hurry because I always give Louise her meds last. All that waiting makes her hate me and she tries to scratch me with her ugly fingernails.

It's lucky that I'm a traveller. I can't waste time on emotion. I have so many places to go.

Most of the children are so beautiful it hurts to look at them. Not Louise. She looks like one of the ugly sisters in

Cinderella. She is thin and pimply, and she makes horrible noises when she tries to talk. And she is twisted all sideways because she has very weak muscles in her back. The braces the orthopedists gave her don't work very well.

Some of the aides like Louise, because she is smarter than some of the other children. She knows some sign language and she goes to school. The teachers run special classes for children with disabilities. They try to communicate with her and spend a lot of time teaching her. She likes the attention. I don't pay attention to her after I give her the meds unless she seems to have a pain.

When Yonatan works here, Louise is a little in love with him. He's gone now, and that's one of the reasons she doesn't like me. When he first comes, people laugh at him behind his back because he is the first male nurse to come to the Center. He can't speak or write English too well and wants to learn in a small private hospital before he tries to get a job in a big city.

I am one of the only people who help Yonatan with his English. We take lunch breaks outside together during the summer. I make flashcards with medical words on them and talk slowly so he can understand.

He learns very quickly. Louise is one of his favorites, and he brings her outside to sit with us while we work. Sometimes he signs with her, and she smiles and makes humming noises under her breath.

Gulie can't sit still outside, so I can never bring her with us. Only Louise comes with us. But after Yonatan's English improves, I tell him that he doesn't have to work here anymore. He gets a much better paying job in the city at a more prestigious hospital where being a male nurse is an advantage.

Louise blames me for telling him he is ready to move on. If I walk by with my cart, she tries to knock some of the medications off so I will get in trouble.

Of course, it's not so simple, Yonatan leaving like that. It also has to do with the long, long hours that you work at the Center, because when the weather is bad, if the next shift doesn't show up, you cannot leave. The children cannot live without us.

A few times Yonatan and I are on duty together for almost twenty-four hours, and things happen. I think maybe some of the other nurses and aides think it was my fault too, that he leaves. They didn't like Yonatan at the beginning, but once he learns more English, they all want to go out with him. He ignores them, of course.

He asks me to come with him when he goes to the new hospital, probably because I am so helpful. And I say no.

If you are attached to someone, it is hard to travel on when you want to. A real traveller is always brave about saying goodbye because the journey is what is important, not the people you meet on it. And that next location could be the one that changes your life.

I am a real traveller. Although sometimes it feels as if everyone else is travelling and I am the only one staying in one place.

I'd rather think about Budapest, on the great river Danube. My mother, my grandfather and my great-aunt come from

Budapest. It's very easy for me to imagine my great-aunt walking down the cobblestones of Heroes' Square, dressed for the opera. That means black, of course, a long black cape and high heels that are thin and menacing, like swords.

I am always polite to waiters but if my great-aunt visits a café, she won't be. I can see her tapping her heels and sending her order back…maybe three times. And smiling, but not tipping, when they get it right.

But that's not real. Do you want to know something real? Once, driving to the Center, I see a mountain goat glaring down at the cars from the top of a stony hill. I think I see it, anyway. There is no one in the car with me, so it could be my imagination.

I crane my neck to look behind me, hoping I can still see the mountain goat's yellow eyes and white beard. But I can't slow down. There is a man in a beard and a baseball cap tailgating me. I'm not such a fast driver even when there's nothing to see.

Maybe I'm going crazy, I think. Maybe next, I'm going to see an angel come down from heaven and give everyone chocolate cake.

But I know that is very different from seeing a mountain goat. A mountain goat is real…isn't it?

Chapter Four

"Adoring a person does not necessarily mean you're happy," said Maria. –Daphne Du Maurier, *The Parasites*

Atlantic City smells like the ocean…Vegas smells like quarters. When you step off the cool dark airplane, you cover your eyes from the glare of the slot machines, only feet away from you in the airport. And then, no matter where you go, you can't get away from them. I think they install them in people's homes. The first thing they do when they get up isn't to make coffee, it's to make quarters. People get used to the chinking sound at all hours. If there is a power outage that silences all the machines, they won't be able to understand each other's words without that sound in the background.

But somehow, money makes this artificial world seem preferable to nature in Nevada. The air is always cool, there are no insects, and none of the dead animals you find by the side of the road in the rest of America. Nothing can be squashed because nothing is alive, everything has been re-placed by automatic slot machines. Everyone is so polite to you because they are only holograms of famous people, not very good ones at that.

Here's a comforting thought: you can't hurt a hologram who has quarters in his chest instead of a heart. It must be a relief to be a health practitioner who works there and doesn't have to worry about feelings, only about money.

I wouldn't live in Vegas, even though this place is a lot less glamorous. One of the good points about working at this hospital is I get to read a lot. We have spells when it is very quiet at night, when I can read and sit by the window. Most of the nurses take turns sleeping when it is quiet, but I like to look outside because there is so little light pollution here. You can watch the stars, and the stars can watch you. And I can read my books without the other nurses trying to see what I am reading.

Sometimes I agree to work a double shift because who is waiting for me at home? Most of the other nurses have families, and they're grateful to me for letting them leave. Especially since this virus started, because some of the nurses are afraid they're going to take it home to their families. I'm not afraid. I know how to hold on to my consciousness. If I do that, I won't die.

The hospital doesn't like to pay overtime, but when there's an emergency, they capitulate. If I agree to take a double shift, I unbraid my hair and put it up in a bun, so it looks as if I went outside and took a break.

It's easy to find a clean set of scrubs, and a clean mask, and

I keep deodorant and scented hand cream in my pocketbook. I wear hand cream because I touch people as I travel from room to room, and I want the touch to be pleasant for them, maybe even something they will remember after they leave the hospital. I make sure my hands are soft and never sweaty or cold. Although now with the virus, we're supposed to wear gloves all the time, making my touch scary and unwelcome. I worry that the gloves don't work, though, so I carry a small bottle of hand sanitizer in my pocket.

Sometimes I stamp my feet a little, walk heavier as I go from room to room to remind myself that I am working. I'm not just here to have fun and encounter new people. After all, I'm a traveller.

Yes, this is a boring college town I've travelled to, and stayed in, but there are some good parts to it, if you know how to find them. If you look at the exterior landscape outside the hospital—the distinct four colors of green you find in the parks as you climb up the waterfalls—you wonder why, in this peaceful college town, do we always have kids trying to commit suicide?

Of course, these particular kids are incapable of seeing anything other than their own clothes, cars, grades—at least, this is what I tell myself so I can stand to take care of them.

Tonight, I special a girl in intensive care. She breaks up with her boyfriend and takes a lot of pills.

She'll be all right. We pump her stomach, and we stay with her even when her family comes, because we don't know what kind of a relationship she has with her parents, whether they will make it worse or better for her.

I try to empty out all my thoughts about such patients, even the parts of my mind that are screaming at them, to look at themselves, young, beautiful and financially secure compared with nine tenths of the world. Isn't that enough, do you have to have complete control over your emotional relationships too, can't you let yourself make a mistake without dramatizing it?

I never say any of that, so I am quite popular as a special. But the girl's parents look at me as though they hate me, because they don't want anyone to know what their daughter has done.

I know quite a few nurses who still believe in God. I don't see how God and death can coexist. Isn't loss of consciousness death? I've seen so many people die, and once that happens, all my ideas about God come up against the facts and crunch. Those other nurses have something I lack, some serene way of twisting reality into philosophy that I can't imitate.

Maybe this virus will change their mind, because it seems as if a lot more people are starting to get sick, and there doesn't seem to be much room for God when that happens.

You'd think the nurses who have children would know better. Once you have a child, you can never escape the fear that something will happen. You'll do anything to keep that connection you made, that one time you reached out of your body and trusted in new life.

That's the problem with getting attached to a child, or a husband, or a cat. It starts out well, but you always regret it in the end. Better not to trust from the beginning.

In case you get it wrong, I don't leave my marriage because Peter does anything to hurt me. He is good in all the ways that I'm bad.

Yes, we live in a box, but I like that at first. I ask Peter to find me a box that is far away from my family, and in a place where I don't have to hear music.

We settle in a remote part of the country where I can listen to birds instead.

At the beginning, Peter tries to take me places with him. He doesn't ask me to stay home in the box. We go on trips to places he thinks I'll find interesting. That's how I get to see the yogi dancing in the graveyard. And there are lots of other places, too. At first, I think that Peter knows what I need and I'm learning a lot.

Until one day I realize the truth. I'm not really travelling when I go to those places, because I see them the way Peter wants me to see them. Never through my own eyes.

To be fair, Peter doesn't know that there is something else wrong with my eyes, something I've never told him, something that changes the way I see the world. Something that has nothing to do with him.

Finally, I tell Peter I don't want to come with him on those trips anymore. He never understands why.

Peter tells me I can buy whatever furniture I want for the box. He wants me to be happy if I stay home.

I don't want any. Why get attached to furniture? Nothing good can come from that. I like the box to be empty, with just a mattress on the floor. I don't even want curtains at the windows.

After Peter realizes I'm not going to change my mind, he buys furniture himself, and I just walk around it most of the time. He begs me to help him choose furniture for the baby's room, but I tell him I will hold the baby when she cries, and the box comes with soft fluffy wall-to-wall carpeting, so we don't need anything else.

At first, when Sara is born, while she is just a baby, I don't mind her crying and the other noises her body made. I don't mind cleaning up her mess. I've always been the one who does that in our family. Peter helps, even when I tell him he doesn't have to.

When we bring Sara home from the hospital, we keep tip-toeing into her room to watch her breathe. If it is raining, I sit on the floor and read to her when she cries. If there is sun, I take her outside and carry her around.

I tell her the names of things, so she won't be the one kid who doesn't know, the way I was.

Peter asks me to invite our relatives over to meet Sara, but I don't see why they deserve to ruin everything. His family only comes once, and it is not a very long visit.

I don't sing to Sara, but Peter does. And I blame him starting Sara on the path to liking music.

It takes a while before I notice Sara has turned into my brother. Of course, I know that once Sara likes music, she won't like me anymore. She deserves to have a better mother.

That's when I leave. But sometimes, I wonder if Peter and Sara miss me.

I miss them.

I'm tempted to believe in karma, if not in actual past lives.

I feel as if I'm paying for leaving Sara without a mother and Peter without a wife.

I wish I had the guts to succeed at just one thing, even something as trivial as a sparkling house. But I start things brilliantly, then just give up. I know it's a pattern. I know I can't stop. It's better to separate myself from all that.

I used to stick my fingers in my ears when my father shouted at my mother. I still do that when I do something wrong, like make a mistake in giving medications. After I get home, I curl up and drink coffee and hide from all of them who are looking at me and talking about me.

At night, here at the hospital, inertia hangs in my head like a hot day—makes me stoop, sweat, stop. It's hard to get up once you sit down. You're reading, someone rings, you know you have to answer, but you resent it, because you haven't moved for almost an hour. It's much easier on the nights when all hell breaks loose and it's as if our bodies are made of coffee.

I sit here, trying to be nice to the others, the nurses and aides because the doctors almost never come by at night. I don't like any of them. I can't be a statue or invisible because I'm getting paid. But I don't feel like I'm a fake, more like a specimen or, better, a diplomat from a foreign world.

Tonight, the other nurses and aides are all older than me and they don't trust me because of the way I look. They think I should cut my hair and get a perm and wear more makeup and get married again. I have to feel my way around them like a blind girl walking down a staircase.

I step around with words. Tonight, one nurse wears the

"down to earth" mask and the other is a "bear." They each have enough self-interest invested in their disguises to prevent them from puncturing mine. And the patients, sunk like seashells in their rooms around the nurse's station, don't care. Or care less. We all care less about each other.

Doctors are strange. Sometimes at market research I can almost enjoy their company, pretend they're human as we sit around a table and snipe at each other. I am at my best then. I like to attack people verbally—it used to make me think I could be a lawyer. Just as I've never had to serve in jury duty and have somehow been taken off that list because people have trouble finding where I live, I have also been required to participate in many focus groups. It is an extra source of income for me, so I don't mind. This is the one time when I enjoy hiding behind my label—I am a nurse, therefore I am valuable to you. Listen!

At my last focus group, where gastroenterologists and nurses mingle as if of one blood, there is a doctor who looks like Santa Claus. He isn't blind to nuances like the others—he is literary, musical, and alert to language.

We craft puns as we sit waiting for the group to begin. But when I ask him why most doctors are so one-dimensional and literal, he is hurt. "I didn't know we were," he says in a puzzled, kind way. I wonder how I missed seeing that he, too, is hiding behind his label—only he is proud of it. I don't talk to him any more after that.

It's so much easier to be silent. I stifle those little voices in my head as I make my rounds.

Even if I protect myself with silence, I still see what others

don't. I'm the invisible watcher at our hospital.
  People, birds, patients. I watch them all.
  If there were dolphins here, I would watch them, too.

45

Chapter Five

But human life does not come back again after it
passes through the fence of teeth.
–Homer, *The Iliad* (translated by Emily Wilson)

Today, I will travel to the Danube River in Hungary. Some of my relatives came from this country. Like an elemental breadknife, the Danube cleaves the city of Budapest into Buda and Pest.

I like the idea of a river having so much power it can tear apart a living, breathing city. But people aren't aware nature is dissecting them. Instead, they stand on Freedom Bridge and watch the sun set over the Danube. I wonder if their reflections in the water even begin to mirror how they feel inside.

I am not in favor of sunsets. I prefer being up early when the sun rises, but I can be flexible while I travel. Since I have limited time on these trips—at any moment, I could be interrupted by an emergency—I am not terribly interested in looking up relatives or cities that may have vanished after World

War II. My main reason to travel to Hungary is to visit the Visegrád Mountains. I want to wait until the Danube is dark and quiet, and then turn away from all the people to hike by myself through the trees. I want to walk slowly and steadily uphill, listening to the wind blow through the trees and watching for birds that I will never see around the Center, such as the Great Bustard, Saker, Imperial Eagle, Pygmy Cormorant, and Ural Owl. I want to memorize the sounds they make when they fly through the forest. If I can do that, eventually, I will be able to reproduce the sounds to others, who may never get the chance to hear them with their own ears.

And if I make a mistake in reproducing the sounds, it doesn't even matter, because I will be quietly making those sounds for children who don't even know what they are, who I am, or what I'm doing.

Today, when I get to the Center, Gulie's family is visiting her. They don't come too often anymore. Her mother looks miserable.

I don't blame her. Imagine that your child is born with red hair and freckles and blue eyes, and at the beginning, you dream that someday, she will become a scientist, or a teacher, or the president of the United States.

But she is a very small baby, and at the hospital, the doctors point out that she has an unusually small head. You don't know what this means. Neither do they, not for sure, because your child is just a baby. The doctors tell you that they are concerned and will watch your child carefully as she grows older.

Your child remains small, maybe because she has trouble

breast feeding, unlike your older daughters. Although her older sisters surround her lavishing awe and love and never-ending attention, she does not respond often. She is very quiet, very small, and she has so many serious health problems.

You have her tested for hearing loss in case her lack of response is just a congenital issue, which seems almost welcome compared to some of the alternatives that begin to surface. Or maybe despite your best efforts, one of her ear infections goes unrecognized, and you blame all your daughter's problems on that.

But each month, more doctors see her and more difficulties are uncovered. She starts to have uncontrollable tantrums, screaming and scratching herself. Tears stream down her face, and you have no idea how to make her feel better. By the time she is three years old, your child is diagnosed with autism and an IQ under 50.

Physically, your child is beautiful. Small and thin, she looks like the child in the Healthtex illustrations. She wears clothes beautifully. She learns to walk, but she doesn't go anywhere, mostly just sits in a corner and hits herself on the head and screams softly.

Later than her sisters, your child learns to walk, and run, but she cannot talk. You think your child can hear, but you have no idea how much of what you say is understood. Eventually, you learn a whole new vocabulary about your child. She has impairments in intellectual functioning, adaptive skills, motor development, sensory functioning and communication skills.

You learn that your child cannot be accommodated in a special education program because her combination of problems is too severe. And definitely, your child, even with a full-time aide, will not receive a public education.

You're told that it will take a lot of work, years of work, for your child to learn to make eye contact, track objects with her eyes, and respond to stimuli around her. Because her disabilities are so severe, it might never happen. It is unlikely that she will learn adaptive self-care skills and will always need help dressing, personal hygiene, toileting, feeding. Behavior will always be disruptive.

At this point, you decide to put your child in a developmental center so that she can get the care she needs. It is not an easy decision. It comes after months of discussion, visits to specialists, desperate searches for alternatives. Her sisters cry at the idea of giving up this child who never responds to them. You have a family meeting in which you all cry, and finally agree to put Gulie in the Center. At first you visit every week, but when you see that there is no chance, no chance at all that she is going to improve, you visit every month, and then, every few months.

When you go to visit your child, you feel guilty that you see her so infrequently, but after all, it's not as if she recognizes you.

Today, Gulie seems mildly amused interacting with her family. Her sisters circle her, give her hugs and kisses that she doesn't return. They speak to her and follow her around the room as she moves from one wall to another.

When she sits down on the floor, they sit down too, but

she barely looks at them. They are all wearing masks, but it really doesn't make any difference because Gulie has no idea who they are or why they are here.

Her mother and I are friends. She knows I love Gulie. She's grateful that someone tries to take good care of her. She's brought more clothes because Gulie is getting taller, even though she is still extremely underweight for her age.

She asks if there's anything else she could bring that might make Gulie happy. I tell her I think Gulie is doing as well as can be expected.

She knows that it's hard to get Gulie to eat and she doesn't seem to have any favorite foods, so she hasn't brought anything except bags of candy. I can usually get Gulie to eat at least a little candy, and it's a good way to distract her so I can get some real food into her mouth while she is looking at it and chewing it, even if she spits some of it out.

Gulie's mother asks why none of the children are wearing masks. I explain that we can't keep the masks on their faces, also Gulie tried to eat hers the last time we put one on. Her mother says that she is frantic because of what she hears about the virus. Her daughters are staying home from school, and she has no idea when they will be allowed to go back to class.

"It's particularly hard on Sam, because she's so gifted," she tells me. I nod, looking over at the bevy of red-haired girls following Gulie around and trying to hug and kiss her even though they must have realized by now she doesn't like to be touched. Sam has Pippi Longstocking braids and round gold-rimmed glasses. Her IQ is off the charts, but she's very gentle with Gulie, taking her cue from Gulie's actions instead of trying to orchestrate them the way her other sisters are doing.

They've brought Gulie a fancy American Girl doll with red hair and blue eyes and beautifully made clothes. They keep trying to show her that the doll looks just like her and therefore she should hold it and play with it. They might as well be invisible.

I used to practice being invisible. I'd sit totally still in class, it wasn't hard. Only my eyes would move, following the teacher writing on the blackboard. I didn't feel as if I were dead, but, sitting still, I'd feel that I didn't exist. Everything about me was moving and I was in the middle, stiff, dumb, not part of it.

Then, when I had to move to get to my next class, I heard people talking around me as though I was still invisible. I saw things I wasn't meant to see and heard things when everyone else stopped listening.

But now, in some ways, it's as if the families who visit are the invisible ones. Now the children sometimes notice me and the other staff, just because we're here all the time and they know what to expect from us, and we have tricks to make them pay attention to us if we try to feed them or give them medicine.

Gulie's mother clutches my arm. "I don't know when I'll be able to visit again. It might be a few months before I can make it back here again. Promise me, Sonia, you'll take good care of Gulie for me."

"I will take care of her," I say seriously, "and I'll try not to let anything happen to her."

I'm still hoping that the virus will skip the Center, since so few people come here. Since the virus started spreading so quickly in the outside world, even in the hospital, more people are ordered to stay home from work and school and even restaurants are closing. I only know this because I saw it on TV at the hospital; I don't ever go to restaurants any more now that Yonatan has left.

"I hope the Center stays open," Gulie's mother says, "because I can't manage taking care of Gulie at home."

"As far as I know, the Center never closes," I reassure her. "And maybe this will all be over in a few weeks."

Because really, how long can people stay home? They're not like me, they'll get so bored. Maybe they'll start driving around town, travelling with nowhere to go. Or read a book. Or bake a cake.

I think people will just drink a lot more alcohol until this is over.

Gulie's mother nods. "Maybe."

She gives the girls a five-minute warning to get ready to leave soon. They're still trying to get Gulie to show some interest in the doll, but she has dropped it and is back to her usual activity of staring at the wall, hitting the side of her head.

The girls put the doll sitting next to her, also looking at the wall. It would be hard to tell the difference between the doll and Gulie if you could not see Gulie's rapid respirations.

The girls hug and kiss Gulie and she makes faint noises as she moves away from them. "Look, she's smiling," one sister says. Gulie does smile sometimes. "You were so glad to see us, weren't you, Gulie?"

And then, finally, they leave and it's just the children and me and the other staff left.

Everyone seems so much happier now because this is the way it's meant to be.

No sunrises. No sunsets. Pretty much the same things every day.

I think the children like it this way.

I know I do.

Chapter Six

A lifetime's accumulation, she thought, of a woman
who had cared about things—things loved for their
color and texture and their associations rather than
their material value.
–Deborah Crombie, *All Shall Be Well*

I think I have time for a quick journey, somewhere…I
know. Madagascar. I'd go to see lemurs, but if I had
enough money, I'd stay at a fancy hotel with a canopy
bed. I saw pictures of the Hotel Sakamanga that look great. It
does say the hotel is mostly for couples, but maybe they
wouldn't mind taking someone who wants to visit the national parks all by herself.

What is it about lemurs that's so appealing? I've always
wanted to see a diademed sifaka. It sounds like an animal
from a fairy tale. They're endangered, so there might not be
all the time in the world to see them. They look like they're
wearing an Alpaca hat. I also want to see the Indri because I

love how their eyes glow. If you're thinking about the gigantic eyes of lemurs, the eyes of angry parents don't seem to matter much. And parents would never be able to climb a baobab tree, but I bet I could. I used to be pretty good at climbing. It's been a long time.

Okay, I admit would never do something like that now. I'd be too embarrassed.

I'm at the hospital. I'm making so much overtime because of the virus. Almost nobody wants to come in, so they wait until the last minute, and then call me to take their shift. If this keeps up, and I am careful and save my money, someday I can take some time off for travel even if I want to stay at a luxury hotel. Only for a few days, just for the experience, so I know what it feels like.

They're bringing us patients we can't help much now. The worst part is their families aren't allowed to be in the room with them. I've never seen anything like this before. Everyone is scared, I mean, not only the patients, but also the medical staff. Well, I'm not scared, but I would be if I thought I had anything to lose.

Being a patient is hard but being a family member is even worse. I know because I remember how terrified I am when my brother has a heart attack a few years ago. I fly to Albuquerque, New Mexico to visit him while he is in the hospital. (He's fine now—he just has to watch his diet and take a statin and some other meds—but it isn't clear at the beginning that he will recover.) I hate flying, and I remember thinking what a waste it will be if my plane crashes, and my brother dies never knowing I take all this trouble to go see him. I don't like my brother, but that doesn't mean I want him to die.

He isn't particularly grateful that I come to visit. Mostly I just bring him fruit, so I have something to eat while I sit in his room and read magazines. We are never going to talk much. I mean, what would we talk about—how much better his childhood is than mine? How he wins the genetic lottery for brains and talent and looks, and I lose?

His wife lets me stay at their house so we can visit the hospital every day until he gets out. The house is sort of interesting because it is made of adobe and has three fireplaces. It's so different from the way houses are built in the East.

I ask my brother's wife to let us use at least one of the fireplaces, but she says it is too hot. So, all I do is go from the house to the hospital and back again at night. I would prefer to visit the Petroglyph National Monument or the National Museum of Nuclear Science, but I think it might be inappropriate to go sightseeing while my brother is so sick.

If he gets sick again, now, I won't be allowed to fly over state lines and I will have to learn about his disease from a distance. That's what it's like now for the families of people with the virus.

Some of these families refuse to leave the hospital; they only desert temporarily to get food and take a shower, then they come back to wait outside in their cars. They're not allowed in the cafeteria anymore because they might raise the risk of infection for us when they take their masks off. I hate walking past them—it feels as if their eyes are burning me.

"Come on, talk to me, Sonia, I'm sooooo bored," Lena groans. I don't know what she wants me to talk about. I've already asked about her boyfriend, and her plans for her days off, and what she's going to do when the hospital grants us a rare three-day weekend. Now I share the brownies I baked because my crumbs are more acceptable than my words.

It seems that when people like Lena—I think of her as a supernatural species of lemur, wearing a jeweled diadem instead of a furry one—are under a lot of pressure, she is incapable of seeing that anything in her life might be temporary and capable of changing tomorrow, including the virus. I wouldn't be surprised if her boyfriend tries to take her away to a place where they think they'll be safe. As if there's such a place.

Lena has an extremely limited perspective about how her life is supposed to unfold—expensive cars, gorgeous clothes, perfect guy. It's not her fault that she is blind to reality; at least, this is what I tell myself so I can stand to work with her. It is not my place to give her advice. I'm only supposed to be Lena's faithful sidekick, her posse who always agrees with her and tells her she looks sensational. But right now, you can't recognize any of us beneath the masks and the paper gowns and the gloves we're required to wear. We're wildly unattractive and we smell like fear.

It's a stressful shift. Four people die on our floor, three from the virus. (I'm not one of those people who says people pass away, or depart; to me, that sounds as if they get to leave the hospital, and if they die, that's not the case.)

Once upon a time, when I am little, I think people had a choice as to whether they have to die or not.

Apparently, I think wrong.

Dying first becomes real to me when I am four years old. I catch a bad cold that will not go away. For weeks, it is hard for me to breathe, and I have trouble sleeping, even propped up with pillows.

My mother gives me purple cough syrup, but it doesn't seem to work very long. Several times a night, I wake up gasping and terrified.

One day I look up at my mother and say, "I'm never going to get better, am I?"

"Of course you are," my mother says. "Soon you can sit in the sun, and it will bake all the germs right out of you."

"What if it doesn't?" I ask. "What happens when people don't get better?"

Of course, she doesn't answer.

When I am a child, I imagine a pill I can take so I will never have to die. By the time I grow old, it seems reasonable to think that doctors will have invented such a thing.

But to my dismay, years pass, and people still die.

I look into ways to avoid death, such as leaving behind a hologram of myself (but it will not be full sized, and it will not have my brain in it).

I even think of being frozen until the right pill comes into the world, but that involves actually dying and trusting that someone will take care of my remains. If no one wants to touch me when I'm alive, who will want to take care of me after I'm dead?

I see my grandparents die, then, when I become a nurse, I see other people die. Each time, especially if someone dies who is close to me, I wonder if they can choose otherwise, choose to keep on living.

With my grandparents, I wonder if they don't love me enough to make this choice. Will they try harder to live, will their choice be different if my brother is in my place?

One of my greatest fears is of dying without being aware that this is happening so that I cannot stop it—being hit by a car, or, by some other method, losing consciousness. It seems to me that if I can only hang on to consciousness, I will be all right.

Maybe some people believe their souls go to a better place, but I can tell you, their bodies are very much left here, and I'm one of the people who have to deal with them. It takes hours, and it takes a long time afterwards to help the families get over their emotions and take the next steps.

"Let's get OWWWWT of here, pleeeeeeeze, Sonia," Lena moans. This is another way the pandemic has affected us. After a bad shift, usually a group of us go out for a drink, or we go to breakfast together after night shift. Especially if there is a bad code, and you feel like shit because you did your job but for whatever reason, the code doesn't work out and the patient dies. But now, we can't spend time together, even if a family collapses with grief on the floor. We have to say, "I'm so sorry for your loss," but we can't touch them anymore.

Do they even register that we're other human beings trying to help them if we can't touch them?

"Hey. Earth to Sonia. Go home and get some rest. We're done." I can tell Lena is smiling at me behind her mask, and she gives me a gloved thumbs up as we retreat to our lockers. Then, in farewell, and not ironically, because she doesn't know what irony is, she gives me an air hug.

I appreciate the gesture. Not that I'm much of a hugger.

In the parking lot, I almost make a mistake. I see a beat-up red Volkswagen, and without thinking, or maybe because I'm tired for once, I put my hand on the door handle, and someone has left the car unlocked. I swing inside before I realize this is not my car, it belongs to someone I don't know, and I have mistaken it for Yonatan's car.

This is an especially stupid thing to do because Yonatan never worked at the hospital, only at the Center.

This is a close one.

Now my legs are shaking, and I have trouble getting out of the car. I slam the door shut and frantically pull my mask down to gulp fresh air. I know my own car is around here somewhere, I just have to get over to it as fast as I can and then I'll be all right.

Chapter Seven

"Bucky, you're shaken by what's happening now, but strong
men get the shakes too. You must understand that a lot of
us who are much older and more experienced with illness
than you are also shaken by it." –Philip Roth, *Nemesis*

There is nothing wrong with being in love with Paris.
Yes, I know it is the city of cliché and no, I would
not go there in April. I don't go there to fall in love
or watch other people who are too weak to know better. But
I love their bookstores and philosophy and poetry and food
and people who ignore me when I'm sitting outside reading
and drinking café au lait.

The best time to travel to Paris is early morning, before the
tourists wake up and come out of their fancy hotels. I go to
Le Marais and stop at the Boot Café for coffee. I plan to keep
walking because it is too crowded inside for me to feel comfortable. Then I head over to the Musée National Picasso-
Paris. I carry a small backpack in case I see something

irresistible in a bookstore.

I'm thinking about Picasso's paintings as I get to the Center, and it takes me a while to stop seeing the children there as figures within paintings. I stop to say hello to Jeff, who is stuffing his hands inside his mouth and laughing.

I nod to Louise, who ignores me. Someone has given her Gulie's new American Girl doll, probably because Gulie has no interest in it.

Louise is holding it tightly now. Ordinarily this would upset me, but instead, today I look at Louise and think how in an alternate universe she could have been a model for a Picasso painting, all angles and masterful lines conveying emotion.

I try to play with Gulie, but something's wrong with her. Gulie is hurting this morning. I can't get her to stop hitting me, and screaming, and there are tears in the corners of her eyes. Her cheeks are pink, and warm to the touch. She won't eat her breakfast.

I get her to stay still long enough so I can take her pulse and temperature. She has a slight fever. I'm sure it's just a cold, worst case strep. But I have to write down her vital signs, and this means I have to give her a COVID test. It's a PCR test that will be sent to the lab, and it will come back in a couple of days, if the lab isn't completely overwhelmed.

What should I do in the meantime? Gulie won't wear a mask, and I don't have a place to put her away from the other children. It would be cruel to make her stay alone in her room, and even if I do close the door, someone will have to stay with her to make sure she doesn't hurt herself.

For a minute, I fantasize about taking her hand and dancing her out the door to the little green Mazda I rent since coming here. Maybe if I put her seatbelt on, she'll be interested enough in the changing scenery to stay relatively still on the drive home. I think about taking her to my tiny apartment and letting her run through all the rooms, touching the shells and fossils that I collect. It would be so nice to be alone with her, not distracted by all the other children here.

It will never work. Gulie will break the shells and swallow my fossils.

I have to tell Steph, the charge nurse, that Gulie is sick. My worst fear is that they will put someone in with Gulie who won't understand her and will tell her to shut up when she screams.

But Steph understands, and she even has a good idea. "You can put her in the craft room," she suggests. "It's closed until Monday, and the therapist can work with the other kids in the main room until we get the test back. We can set up shifts so someone can stay with Gulie."

"We can tell the cleaners to be extra careful when they disinfect the rooms tonight," Jenna adds. She's one of my favorite aides at the Center. I've seen a few of the aides get rough with the children when they think no one is watching, but Jenna would never do that. She's not pretending to be kind to keep her job, she is kind.

I take water and sandwiches and cookies and diapers and get ready for the first shift with Gulie in the craft room. She doesn't seem to realize that she's being shut away from all the other children when we first go in there. She's too busy looking around and pulling open all the drawers that contain the art supplies. She loves spilling everything out.

Destruction and mayhem keep Gulie busy for a while, so that I can sit and stick food under my mask and get acclimated to the room.

When the floor is covered with pencils and markers and stickers, Gulie loses interest. She goes to the door and tries to open it, but of course it doesn't move.

Gulie spends about ten minutes trying to escape, then seems to accept that she has to stay in the room. She goes back to her usual behavior of constantly moving around the room, screaming softly to herself and pulling her beautiful red hair or hitting herself on the side of the head. Sometimes she picks something bright colored off the floor, carries it around for a while, then drops it and seems to forget about it.

Gulie even comes over to me and stands in front of me, looking at the food I have brought. I try to get her to eat, but I think her throat is sore and it is hard for her to swallow.

I pick Gulie up and sit her on my lap so that I can give her some water from one of the bottles I brought in here, and she does drink a little.

Then she turns her head into my shoulder for a moment, a very short moment of being still. It is almost as if she is saying thank you. I know better, but when we're alone like this, it's easier for me to pretend that Gulie is normal, or almost normal.

Then Steph opens the door to check on us. Gulie runs over and tries to get out.

"Not happening, little one," Steph says, barely registering

that Gulie is hitting the door over and over. "How's it going in here? I had to call her parents and tell them she has a fever."

I swallow. "Gulie's good. She drank a little water. I can't get her to eat, though. Steph, I'm worried because her mother and the girls were here last week. Are any of the other girls sick?"

Steph shrugs. "I spoke to her mother. She said the other girls are fine, so hopefully, they'll stay fine."

"I don't think the mother will come even if Gulie has to be hospitalized," I say. I watch Gulie sit down on the floor and rock back and forth. "Last week, she said she doesn't know how to take care of Gulie at home, and she's afraid for the other daughters. Should I stay with her tonight?"

"Of course not," Steph says. "Come on, it's not as if she even knows you're here. We'll put her in her room when it gets dark, and I'll have an aide stay with her until she falls asleep and check on her through the night. She'll be fine."

I nod. As long as Gulie hasn't somehow picked up coronavirus, theoretically she won't get too sick. I'm most worried about her getting dehydrated.

"I'll give the meds out after lunch," Steph offers, "so you can stay with her until your shift ends."

"Steph, what are we going to do if they all get sick?"

"I honestly don't know," Steph says, "so let's hope it doesn't happen."

I know a nurse who used to work here until she got married and moved to Amsterdam. She sends me emails now, and this week, she told me the city is on lockdown. Even in people's homes, only four adults and four children are allowed to gather at one time. This would be hard if, say, you were trying to give a birthday party. But we have far more than four adults and four children here at the Center, and not enough staff if too many people get sick all at once.

It would be best if we tried to keep them here, rather than send them to the hospital. I would be especially uncomfortable about children from the Center coming to the hospital and crossing my two worlds so I might never get to separate them again. But it may not be possible for everyone to stay here. I try to think about Amsterdam and all the museums there, probably empty now, but for some reason, I don't feel like travelling right this minute.

Steph leaves to administer meds, and this time, Gulie doesn't even bother to try to follow her. She's lying on her back on the floor now, staring at the tiny holes in the ceiling. I wish I had some kind of mobile to put up there for her, and then I realize I am surrounded by practically every art material in the universe. So I construct something shiny and glittery, like a universe made by someone who wouldn't look twice at a black hole, and I hang it over Gulie's head. Only now, she won't look at it.

I know I can't bring her home, but if there was a way to smuggle in my cat, I would. I think she would enjoy touching her fur, hopefully not pulling it. My cat has very soft white fur and big paws. They feel like leather when you gently run your fingers across the bottom side. To be honest, though, we've had specially trained dogs come in and Gulie never paid any attention to them, even when they stood next to her and gently licked her cheek. I'm not sure Gulie even knows what an animal is.

I think a good toy for Gulie might be one of those Fur Real stuffed animal cats that purr and meow and open and shut their eyes as long as the batteries are working. If she accidentally hurt that kind of toy, it wouldn't matter. It makes me think of the not alive, not dead Schrodinger's cat.

I change her diaper, and she doesn't resist much. When she is clean and dry, she runs around the room again, but I can see she is finally getting tired. I find some bolts of felt and unroll them on the floor. I know I should keep her awake, but I'm getting tired too, so we both sit down on the felt, and rest for a few minutes.

This is definitely the best day I have had all week. I wonder why it's so much easier for me to spend time with Gulie than with other people. Is it because she has no idea who I am, and no desire to judge me? Or is it because I have all the control here? I would like to think it's because I am a nice person who cares for her, but I know I am not that nice.

The truth is that Gulie doesn't ask much of me, in fact, she doesn't ask anything.

Chapter Eight

To conceive of such a luxury, you needed an
American mind.
–Hanya Yanagihara, *A Little Life*

There's a children's book called *The Phoenix and the Carpet* by E. Nesbit. I always wondered what happened to the carpet. I like to think it might be in the Turkmen Carpet Museum in Ashgabat, Turkmenistan on 5 Gorogly Street. Since 1994, this museum has exhibited the most amazing carpets, all made by hand, mostly woven by women. I wish I lived on 5 Gorogly Street. It sounds so twisted.

I'd love to travel there and find the magic carpet from the book. I think I could walk through the rooms learning how to hand knot and pick compatible colors. I'm always looking for patterns, though it's much easier to see them in a carpet than in real life. I would peer at one carpet after another, and I like to think that suddenly, I would see my special carpet and recognize its powers.

It seems to me that creating a carpet is like creating a baby, because no two are ever alike. So, you must be a great artist to make a carpet, and it would be an honor to be asked to weave one to mark a special occasion. A woman might create a new carpet for a wedding present, or to commemorate a death, or when a child is born.

Currently at this hospital, if we wove carpets in addition to taking care of sick people, all the carpets would commemorate deaths. It's been that way for a couple of months now, and there is no sign that things will get better.

We're all working double shifts now, and sometimes they evolve into triple shifts because there's no guarantee the next shift will come in. Everyone's terrified and almost everyone calls in.

I don't call in. Therefore, I'm greatly in demand.

I've been working with Sharon for the past sixteen hours. She's not exactly one of my favorite people, but her replacement didn't make it in, so she's stuck here with me, and not too happy about it.

I do think I owe my colleagues and my patients the courtesy of at least trying to freshen up between shifts. I've changed my mask and paper gown, combed my hair, and applied deodorant. Underneath my gloves, my hands are soft and fragrant with hand cream. This is my way of showing patients that I respect them in case I am the last person a patient sees and smells and feels.

Sharon doesn't feel this way, though. She wants everyone to know that she's been here way too long and it's against her will. So, she won't change her gown even though I've pointed out it's the worse for wear, and her hair is coming undone, and even her mascara is smearing because everyone knows it doesn't last for twenty-four hours but she insists on wearing a lot of it anyway.

Tonight, most of my patients are doing relatively well, considering how severe this virus is, but one is old and very, very fat and in bad shape. I doubt he'll last the night. I am spending more time in his room than I should.

Sharon is in a bad mood now, and she keeps calling me to come and help her. She's not so great at coming to help me. The last time we were in my patient's room together, we had to do cardiopulmonary resuscitation, and I thought Sharon was doing it too fast, and I yelled at her, "slow down, do it right!" But he started breathing again on his own, and she flounced out of the room. Now, if I call her again, there's a risk she'll pretend she doesn't hear me.

Every time Sharon works overtime, she can't stop thinking about all the extra minutes she is exposed to the virus, and how terrible it would be if she brought it home to her family. She has a two-year-old daughter who looks just like her. She even wears the same sparkly earrings and frizzy perm. No mascara, yet, though, because two-year-old girls smear makeup all over their faces. But as soon as she's old enough, there will be mascara because Sharon is of the opinion that anyone can be beautiful if they put enough effort into changing their natural appearance.

I am wasting time thinking about Sharon because I would rather not think about what's happening here at the hospital and how the virus has taken over. This is a good time to think about travelling, but just right now I don't want to think about weaving yet another carpet as a memorial to yet another death.

Tonight, I think about India. It's less than 1800 miles from Turkmenistan. The Bharatpur Nature Conservatory near Delhi is where the endangered Siberian crane winters. This exceptional bird can be seen in February and March. I don't think my fat patient can hear me anymore, but just in case, I recommend this to him: before your spirit leaves this earth, travel to India with me. Share my binoculars so we can watch the crane walk by the water.

Despite my best efforts, this hospital has become a place where people travel to die, and sometimes this comes between me and my own travelling. I try not to mind it so much. My methodology is to find something else to concentrate on. And, miraculously, I find Sharon. She's standing in front of me, hissing, "Get 619's vitals, now!"

Even if I have uncharitable thoughts, I can't possibly hurt Sharon. She gets mad at me, but she always forgives me because she thinks I have the most beautiful hair in the hospital. "If only you would let me give you a makeover," she'll say when we have a minute to ourselves, "I could make you look so hot!" She never stops to wonder why I always have my hair braided and wrapped around my head so no one can see how long it is. If people knew what I really look like, with my hair down, they would grab it like a handle and cut it off. And then I would lose all my power.

In a moment of madness, I once promised to go to

Atlantic City with Sharon when the pandemic is over. Sharon loves to gamble. I can't stand it. If I won by mistake, I would have to give it all away. Well, Sharon would take it, she loves money.

The real problem is that I am not sure what would happen to me if I went on a real trip. By myself, I mean, because travelling with Sharon would be like travelling by myself. Would all the details of the places I have travelled in my mind leave my head and never come back? Would I turn into a different person, one who goes places and does things? I mean, think of Turkmenistan and India. In my mind, the distance between them is nothing, but how would I manage if a trip became a reality?

No, I can't imagine that. And perhaps the pandemic will never be over, or Sharon will forget my promise, and a real trip to anywhere will never happen.

But now there is a code in room 619, and I have to put myself into action. After forty-five minutes, one of the doctors calls time of death, and we can all stop moving. Except I don't seem to want to stop. Sharon has to take my arm and pull me away from the patient. What is this all about?

"Sonia," Sharon says to me, "take a break."

"I'm fine, I don't need a break," I answer.

"Yes. You do."

She guides me outside the room to the hallway and forces me to sit down in one of the chairs in an empty room. A lot of our rooms are empty now. I think she's being ridiculous, but then I realize my hands are shaking, so I sit for a few minutes and take deep breaths and try to get my shit together.

I think it's because tonight, I've had enough of death. I mean, come on. Why can't there be just one night without anyone dying?

I want to go back to the days when everyone was having annoying elective surgeries, all canceled now. In those days, my major concern was to reassure patients about anesthesia, or assure them that their wound was healing nicely, and that they would be able to leave the hospital in only a few days. I remember when I was more worried about people living and complaining that the hospital food was suboptimal than about people dying.

I mean, it happened, the dying, but not often enough to bother me.

I should have appreciated those days more.

I've regained my composure, so I go back into the room. Now, the doctors leave to return to their nice comfortable beds, and Sharon and I have to disengage all the tubes and intravenous needles. There's a lot to clean up.

She takes care of restocking the crash cart so it's ready for the next patient. I am in charge of getting rid of all the fluids and semi-solids that come out of a patient in the process of death. Because it is a process. There's not just one dramatic moment, no matter what it looks like on TV. Trust me, you have to be there.

We used to let the family come in after the patient was cleaned up but now, we tell them by phone. Sharon will do that part. She has a gentle, sympathetic manner and she's good at lying and saying there was no pain, or even that someone said goodbye. After all, it doesn't make any difference to the patient, and it makes the family feel a little better. Maybe.

No one really knows how long the virus lasts after death, so for now, most family members can't even be present at funeral services. This patient survived World War II, so there will be a military funeral; but no one will be allowed to attend. Sometimes there is a video.

Amazingly, it is still the middle of our shift, and Sharon and I will have to go through this all over again at least once or probably twice, until the night is over.

There's another welcome distraction when one of the doctors asks me about my very fat patient. I lead her to his room and thankfully, he is still breathing.

The doctor checks his vitals and asks me some questions about how he's doing. I tell her I doubt he'll make it through the night.

I know I should feel more comfortable with this doctor because she is a woman, but I don't. It's not that I'm jealous or don't respect her expertise. Gender aside, I don't trust any of the doctors. They're like another species that feeds on the nurses. On the evening and night shifts, when I work, they come and go. They're good for writing the orders, but that's different from spending time with the patients. If they knew the patients better, they'd realize the futility of writing most of those orders.

I'm a little surprised when I realize this patient has just died and this doctor is crying.

In my mind, I'm travelling with this patient and we're bird watching. But then I snap out of it because how did I forget it's the middle of summer. Everyone knows by the time summer comes, the Siberian crane has migrated away from the Conservatory. A crane is not like a pet that you can always keep with you.

When my old cat Charley died, I had him cremated and now I have his ashes in a small wooden box. I try not to be attached, but I don't want to let him go, because then I'll really be alone.

If I ever get to go to the Carpet Museum, or the Bharatpur Nature Conservatory, I will not leave Charley behind. I will take him with me.

Chapter Nine

"We neatened it just the other day," she said. "It has no *right* to burn." –Shirley Jackson, *We Have Always Lived in the Castle*

Mount Spurr, a volcano in Alaska, is over eleven hundred feet high. Its indigenous name is K'idazq'eni, which means "that which is burning inside."

Burning, just the way I am. If I was born with superpowers, I would have been Lava Girl. I would use my powers to tell when a volcano would erupt and save people before their emotions—I mean their lava—spurts out and buries the earth. I would know to look past the calm surface to the heat that, at any moment, can come boiling out.

If I could start over, I would be a volcanologist and understand structural geology.

I tell myself that being a nurse is like being a volcanologist for humans instead of mountains, but it's not true. It's probably more useful to be a volcanologist for mountains.

Gulie travels too, but of course, not the way I travel. She flits from one room to another, never sitting still, never connecting her movements with what is inside her head. This is the mark of Gulie—this morning, for thirty seconds, while she is a screaming captive in her highchair, I get her to crumple some paper instead of pulling her hair. It makes her laugh between screams. I'm going to keep the paper.

Gulie still has a fever, and she's still coughing, but the COVID test came back negative. I'm still suspicious. I hope it wasn't a false negative. Gulie is so happy to be wandering around the Center again that it would kill me to lock her up in one place for being sick. I hope no one else gets sick.

I'm filling out Gulie's chart and at the same time watching the food service worker prepare the meals. I think he's tripping behind his mask—eyelids all fluttery, showily pulling the shells off the eggs as if they contain God. I make toast for everyone—he can't, he burns it three times. Before breakfast I see him lying on a table by the machines. It's hard to get used to these shifts, so I'm not going to complain about him yet. Besides, he looks like the starving, sensitive type. He won't last long here.

Gulie licks my knee. She gets a funny sarcastic glint in her eye sometimes, as if she almost knows me. As if all this motor activity, this screaming, is only an act. Well, that's Gulie. Acting weird to keep people away from her. No wonder we like each other.

The continuing problem we have at the Center is that barely any of the children will wear masks. We can't keep the ones who can walk apart from each other. Now that she's not in isolation anymore, Gulie pirouettes through the rooms, she cannot be contained, and there are at least a dozen other children like her. We can manage the children in the wheelchairs a tiny bit better, and position them at least six feet apart, and put masks on their faces, but some of them are frightened and some of them think it's funny to take the masks off.

We carry around a lot of disinfectant. There are way fewer visitors than usual; I don't know when we'll see Gulie's sisters again. I don't blame them; I know they must think of her and worry about her. Some of the children used to get care packages, but now everything has to be opened and disinfected, and if relatives are sending food, I am not sure it ever gets to the children.

At least now we have tests, and we test every day, and when someone gets sick, they are isolated. It doesn't mean they are left alone in there. I mean, the Center is not a hotel. These children cannot ring a bell, hoping someone will answer. We have to ring the bell for them. I haven't been with anyone in isolation yet, though, except for Gulie.

There are too many meetings lately in which we talk about what will happen if all the children get sick. If too many get sick, the Center will have to close. So far, we can remain open, but at some point, a more transmissible variant may force everyone to take their children home. This will be bad for many of the children because I'm not sure how their parents can take care of them. I am afraid some of them will be taken to another hospital or place like the Center, and then I will never see them again.

Gulie and Jeff are tested every day because they're at such

high risk, but so far, they are not sick with anything more than a bacterial infection (at least, I think that's what Gulie has. It's a bit hard to tell). It's something of a miracle. They both touch everything and everyone, and their hands go in their mouths every minute.

I test myself too. I am not sick. I wash a lot, and I am very good about wearing a mask. If one of the children pulls it off my face, I immediately get a new one.

I lose some weight, but that is because I am worried about the children. I am not sick. If I don't feel like eating, that doesn't mean I am sick.

Losing weight is like travelling. You keep moving, you keep thinking of the one you love. As long as you think of Yonatan, you will be light. I lose twelve pounds in three weeks when I meet him. It is easy.

It is supposed to be nonprofessional to fall in love with someone you work with. The aides and the nurses tell me this when Yonatan came. If it's true, why are they all in love with him, too?

There are some things that are more important than our jobs, and we all want them and are ready to throw away our lives for them. And that is why we each have a story of folly, deceit, and suffering.

Yonatan and I write ours together.

In the first two months, before he says anything, they all whisper about him in the hallways. They dress for him; they live for him. I am the only one who ignores him because I never think he is interested in me.

He came to the Center on a cold day in February when

everything was frozen. I was on the floor with Jeff and Gulie and Thomas when he first came in. I haven't said anything about Thomas before because his story is different from the stories of most of the other children. It hurts me to think about Thomas. I'll talk about him later.

I notice Yonatan seems more alive than the others. But I am not interested. It takes days before he talks to me, and then, I think he is only being kind to show how superior he is to the others.

After I know him better, I realize that Yonatan is never kind.

We only speak to each other about work. He says that the first time he knows he loves me was when he hears me telling Gulie a story after she rocks herself into a screaming fit. I am holding her hands to keep her from hitting herself in the head and she start laughing. I quiet her down by telling her the story of Pippi Longstocking. I tell her she looks just like Pippi, and she laughs as if she can understand me, although every laugh ends in a faint scream.

Most of the aides turn away from Gulie when they realize there is nothing about her they can hold in their hands and get credit for, nothing they can point to and say they changed and made her better.

Gulie's body gets a little older each year, but her brain doesn't develop. Yonatan says he likes people who never change. He likes Gulie for what she is, because despite how she acts, she is someone unique and special, a someone of her own. He makes me see her on her own terms, instead of as a distorted scream of a child, the way the aides see her.

Everyone knows that Yonatan likes me before I do. I think he only talks to me to get closer to Gulie.

She does seem to like him. She runs after him through the halls and tugs at his pockets.

I almost feel jealous, because I can never move and make it look as if I am dancing, the way Gulie does. I have good rhythm in my legs, but my shoulders are stiff, as if I am only half a person and something is missing on top.

And all this time, while Yonatan is starting to love me, and I am starting to love him, I think about Peter. How before I left him and met Yonatan, our marriage has become a habit, but maybe, it is a good habit that should not end. A habit that could start again and live a long healthy life if I go back to Peter. Instead of staying here.

We are kind to each other alone and in public. I have a daughter, I have him, and why, why isn't that enough?

I am not sure that replacing Peter with Yonatan will solve the root of the problem.

When I am home at my apartment, I pretend that nothing is happening inside me and refuse to think about work. And when I am at work, I only think about the children. I pretend that any attention Yonatan shows me is purely because I care so much about the children.

I still go to bed at night thinking of Peter, and I still get up in the morning and put on my scrubs and go to work. Oh, it goes without saying, I also put on my I-am-separated from my family-do-not-ask-me-about-myself mask. Not a paper one. The virus comes later.

The first time Yonatan kisses me, I get up and walk away.

I think it is a mistake. He tells me later that he does, too. I ask him why he doesn't find someone who is prettier than me, and not married. I tell him this is wrong, and he is causing me anguish.

He says, "It's worth it."

And he asks me to leave my husband and come to live with him instead. You can only say such things if you are handsome and smart and strong, and entirely confident of your effect on women.

I am amazed when he says it, because I see Yonatan with some of the other women, the ones who like him because of the size of his cock. But this feels different.

I have the experience of being so in love with someone that your body feels like flames when you press up against each other. The problem is, when does that experience justify the pain that you can cause other people? Does it ever?

Is adultery something that is a concept in books, an outdated concept that has lost all its power? Maybe it doesn't really count anymore, in this age when money and status are all that matter, not religion?

If you are married to the wrong person and you decide to break your lives in half, and separate from the ties that bind you together, will this hurt your soul forever?

No one seems to know the answers, and for once, when I read, it doesn't help me. It doesn't help me to travel either, because I am just carrying these problems from one country and time to another.

I carry Thomas around with me, too. I can only tell his story in a rush to get it out of my head. In another country, far, far, away, a tiny infant is born with several different conditions, and in particular one known as spinal muscular atrophy. His muscles are weak and floppy, and doctors tell his family that he will need a lot of care. His family brings him to the Center when he is six months old, and then they flu far away, and we never see them again. We name the baby Thomas.

So now Thomas lives here at the Center. We love him and feed him and take care of him. He will always be tiny, and he will never talk or move beyond opening and closing his eyes and turning his head. But he loves music and ice cream, and we take him on field trips in a special wheelchair padded with soft sheepskin next to his sensitive skin. He can't sit upright by himself, but he's one of the few children who can wear a mask. I'm relieved we can protect him at least in this way.

Sometimes Gulie dances over to Thomas and just stands next to him.

Sometimes Jeff rolls over to Thomas and wants to hug him, but Jeff is too strong, so we try to teach him to pet Thomas gently instead. We think Thomas likes the attention from the way he squinches up his eyes when Jeff comes close.

Thomas, Jeff, and Gulie are my favorites because they need me the most.

Chapter Ten

I wanted to help her see the value of her adventure.
–E.L Konigsburg, *From the Mixed-up Files of Mrs. Basil E. Frankweiler*

When I travel, I can't help learning about history, even though sometimes I'd rather not know these things. I've learned there are good emperors and bad emperors. I'd rather bleep over the bad ones and learn about the good ones. Suleiman the Magnificent, for example—how could anyone be bad with a name like that? Also, in the pictures I've seen, he had a very attractive well-tended beard, although he probably had an army of servants to trim it for him.

Suleiman was a poet, not just an emperor, so I like to think of him reading and maybe applauding the poet-musicians who travelled around the Ottoman Empire and performed for him. I hope he wasn't jealous if their poetry was a lot better than the stuff he wrote. I wouldn't mind reading

Suleiman's poetry sometime, in translation.

So today, in honor of the good emperors, not the bad ones, I travel to the Albanian Alps. My plan is to follow a trail through Thet National Park. It's not the season to go snow-shoeing there, but I can pretend to be a student and go camping. I'd like to get one of those pop-up tents because I love the idea of carrying my house around with me like a turtle.

I mean, why not? It's summer and my apartment is stiflingly hot. I have one tiny air conditioner in my bedroom, but I only turn it on at night. It's so much cooler at the hospital I don't even mind working double shifts there. I used to insist on having one free day a week, Friday, so I could rest and get ready to work at the Center on the weekends, but now my schedule is shot to hell because of the virus.

The air is so clean here in the mountains. It's much cooler than my apartment, and way more comfortable than the hospital. I've heard there are little villages, and it might be nice to see people who actually live here as I climb through the peaks and valleys. But I don't know how to say hi or ask for coffee, so I'll just make do with my freeze-dried instant instead. It doesn't taste so bad because the water is so clean here.

I'm okay with not seeing bears and lynx and wolves, but I'd like to catch a glimpse of a roe deer or a selvage goat. They're both other-worldly creatures that look as if they've escaped from fairy tales. There are supposed to be three different kinds of woodpeckers here, too. Not sure if I can tell them apart, not from the sound in trees, anyway.

Before I can really lose myself in the quiet and the fresh air, Margaret asks me to chase down this woman who has locked herself into the bathroom again.

Margaret and I have been working together more than usual the last couple of weeks. She's older than some of the other nurses and divorced and living alone, like me.

For Margaret, the virus doesn't have the supernatural powers some of the other nurses ascribe to it. In her own words, "COVID is just one more shitty thing to deal with at work."

Also, Margaret doesn't pester me like the other nurses about my dating life, so I don't mind talking to her so much. Even though I'd rather keep hiking in Albania, I force myself to smile and nod.

On the fourth floor there are two public bathrooms. Homeless people seem very interested in using our bathrooms. They like to stroll through our hallways as if they're mall walking. We don't get as many during night shift, but some of them have learned we don't have as many security guards at night, and somehow, they sneak through.

About once a week, someone locks the door of one of the bathrooms and refuses to come out until they get hungry. We were tolerant of this behavior until the virus, but we can't have extra people walking around anymore. Now, just breathing on someone or something could be dangerous.

For a minute, I think about this, and it appalls me. The only thing to do is not think about it and follow orders.

I'm used to homeless people. When I worked in a library, it was my job to kick them out at the end of the day. I learned how to be firm, but nice about it. So now I knock on the bathroom door and do the same thing.

I can always call security if I have to, but today I don't. The door slowly opens and a stooped over elderly lady emerges after only fifteen minutes of cajoling.

Her face is walnut colored and wrinkled. It could be from dirt because whatever she was doing in the bathroom, it wasn't washing. She smells like a mixture of sweat and body odor and urine and feces, but I don't let on.

She's wheeling one of those upright grocery carts you can buy at Stop N' Shop, using it as a walker because she can't stand upright without support. It's full of all her possessions, mostly tattered blankets and old clothes from the look of it. Nothing valuable, except to her.

So here I am, wearing my mask and paper gown and gloves, looking like an alien from a space opera, and here she is, looking way more normal than I do, but I have to tell her that she can't come here anymore.

"I'm sorry, but you need to leave right now, and you can't come back," I say.

She blinks at me. "You got any money?"

"I'm sorry, I don't have any money," I reply. I do have money, but it's locked up behind the nurse's station and I can't get to it until after my shift. "This isn't personal, I'm just doing my job, but you can't come here any more because of the virus. You need to leave right now."

"Just some spare change? I'm hungry, I need food."

I swallow. "I can call the shelter to try to get you a bed for tonight."

"Why you think I'm here? No beds at the shelter."

"You can't stay here," I say gently. "It's because of the virus. You have to go outside. And you can't keep coming back here. It's too dangerous."

She just looks at me.

"How did you get in?" I ask. "Didn't you see the signs about the virus? You're not allowed to be here anymore. No one is, except for staff and patients. No more visitors. Not even family members."

"My husband died," the woman says. "On July 27, 2012. I'm all alone."

She's so specific about when the tragedy in her life started, it ends me. I can't play by the rules anymore.

"I'm sorry," I say again. "I'm so sorry."

But it isn't enough to be sorry. I remembered a horrible moment of childhood, when I accidentally slammed the cage door on my friend's infant raccoons. I can still see them startle and hear them moan in their sleep. There's enough harm in the world. I can't bear to cause harm without meaning to.

"Look, how about…no, this is what we'll do."

She continues to look at the ground. Not at me, because she can't raise her head.

"You can't stay here. I'll have to call security if you stay here. But if you agree to go outside, I'll get you some money. You can wait for me on the bench outside the main entrance. You know, the one by the tree and the flowers."

She looks skeptical.

"You can trust me," I say. "I'll try to come sooner, but you might have to wait a while. But I'll come before it gets light outside."

She considers me, then nods and begins to shuffle toward the glass doors.

"No, not that way, you'll get caught," I warn her. "I'll take you out through the basement." I press my access card to the elevator, and it opens, empty of course, because hardly anyone is here anymore.

I hold the elevator door while she slowly maneuvers her shopping cart inside, the smell so much worse in the enclosed space that I breathe through my mouth, turning my head so she doesn't see.

From the basement, I watch her step by step making her way to the very unwelcoming metal bench. She can't lie down on it because it's designed to discourage people from spending the night there, with vertical barriers that dissect the bench into three secluded nooks. But she can sit there, uncomfortably, until I access what she needs.

Margaret raises her eyebrows when I return to the nurse's station. "You took long enough."

"I got her out, but she didn't want to go," I answer. "I promised her some money. Do you have any money? I only have a twenty in my purse."

"What? That's plenty, if you're giving her your own money."

I glare at her. "It will barely buy her a few meals. She can't buy supplies to cook her own food. She's homeless, her husband died, now she can't come here and there's no other place for her to go."

Margaret doesn't start crying or anything, but I see her expression change.

"Just wait."

She goes into the room where we lock up the drugs (we

change the passcode every night and there's a silent alarm, so don't even think of trying anything). She comes back holding a roll of bills. I goggle.

"It's from the discretionary fund," Margaret says, deadpan. "You never saw it. Give it to her."

Once again, I take the elevator to the basement, find the woman sitting watchfully outside her shopping cart and hand her the money. She doesn't say anything.

I didn't expect a blessing, but nothing? Then I realize by taking the money, she's helping me. For once, I'm doing the right thing.

It feels strange. I have to think about why I almost never feel this way anymore. Not since I left Peter and Sara. And whether I want to feel this way more often.

"You need to leave now," I say, "and don't come back. Take these too. You should be wearing one now. Don't forget."

I hand her some masks from the box that we keep inside the lobby, and she tucks them into her shopping cart and rises from the bench.

Even though I have to go back inside and finish my shift, I feel like an emperor. One of the good ones.

Pandemic Phase Two
(July through October 2020)

Chapter Eleven

"That's more or less what I imagined had happened," I said. "You see, I was right; you cut her throat as surely as if you'd drawn the knife across it with your own hands."
–Somerset Maugham, *The Razor's Edge*

I'm fond of visiting castles. They make me feel as if I am in a fairy tale.

Today, I am travelling to the town of Aberystwyth in Wales. They have a castle (it's ruined, but so what). They also have the National Library of Wales, and even a seafront. I wish I had relatives there, so I could visit every year. I'd like to get to know Aberystwyth as well as I know my town in Pennsylvania, where they don't have most of the things that I like.

In Aberystwyth, I can pick out books at the National Library even if they don't let me take them out. I can at least write down some promising titles and look them up later on my computer. Then, at the castle grounds, I can walk through history while I imagine men in armor riding horses. I can pretend I lived there a long time ago.

Or I can watch birds on the Royal Pier. I'll skip arcade games and bowling and ice cream, but I might take a ride on the Cliff Railway. I hate the noise of automobile traffic, but I love the whistle of a train. When I hear it, I feel at home.

I'm up early this morning travelling because I work at the Center today. Just thinking about it makes me feel more relaxed than when I know I have to work at the hospital.

I have a rare night off on Friday. I watch a movie starring Lily Gladstone on Apple TV. I treat myself to Thai takeout, even though I'm trying to save money for my trip. I love peanut sauce, and my cat does, too. I put the leftovers in her bowl.

Going to bed is torture for me because I can never relax. But I've been working so much overtime that I build up a sleep deficit. I fall asleep pretty much the minute I put my head down, instead of tossing and turning for hours. I sleep until the sun coming through the shades woke me up this morning.

I remember this feeling. I haven't felt it for a while. I'm happy.

I make two cups of French roast coffee because I don't know what kind of coffee they drink in Wales. Probably they drink tea. I don't know what kind of breakfast they eat in Wales, either. But there will be plenty of food at the Center if I'm hungry later.

After I feed my cat, I sit in my tiny living room on the Ikea sofa surrounded by shelves overflowing with books and fossils. It's peaceful. Quiet. Sometimes I can hear my neighbors playing music late at night, but that means they get up late on the weekends. I have the apartment all to myself for now. I can concentrate on travelling.

I spend about an hour imagining taking a tour of the Aberystwyth castle. Oh, how I'll torment the guide! Everyone will wonder who I am, asking intelligent questions, alone and mysterious. I'll wear black. It contrasts with my hair. I always wear black when I'm not in scrubs.

Then my cell phone rings. It's charging in my bedroom, so I have to run in there to catch whoever's calling.

It's Steph from the Center, asking me to come in early. "We're calling an emergency meeting," she says. "Can you get here by eight a.m.?"

I'm mystified, but I agree to come in early. I can cut my castle tour short.

As always on a weekend, there's not much traffic. I arrive a little early at the Center. But the drive makes me tense, despite my good night's sleep and relaxing start to the morning.

It's a cloudless morning with just enough breeze to make me want to buy balloons filled with helium and set them free before I go into the Center. And that makes me remember the perfect day years ago when I drove to the Center and made the mistake of feeling happy early in the morning. That day turned out to be 9/11.

Today isn't worse, but it's right up there.

When I go inside, most of the nurses are already there, sitting in the small conference room that we use for talks with families. There's not enough room for all of us to have a seat at the table. I'm happy to take one of the plastic seats that run around the edge of the room. We use them for extra seating once a week when we show movies. Usually, someone puts a supersized box of doughnuts in the middle of the table, but not today. This is not that sort of meeting.

Steph is at the head of the table, in one of the upholstered swiveling chairs. She looks unusually serious. She nods at me when I come in.

"Are we waiting for anyone else?" I ask. It seems weird that there are no aides in here with us. I can see them looking at us through the conference room, trying to look as if they're not looking.

"No, let's get started," Steph says. "There's no easy way to say this. I found Jeff with a broken arm this morning."

There's a collective gasp. I feel sick.

"Do we know how it happened?" someone asks. "Is it on video?"

There are cameras in all the rooms, but after you've worked here a while, you learn how to avoid them. No one can be smiling and pleasant on video for eight hours nonstop. And imagine trying to keep that up on a double or triple shift.

"It's not on video," Steph says. "I found him crying in bed. He's been taken to the hospital for x-rays and to get a cast on his arm."

"Is it a bad break?" I ask.

"Yes, it's bad." Steph looks around the room at all of us. "Has anyone noticed anyone having a problem with Jeff? I know he can be violent without meaning to be, but until today, I thought everyone knew how to handle him."

Meena clears her throat. "Are we sure Jeff didn't fall? Or hurt himself accidentally in some way? He's very strong."

"It wasn't an accident," Steph says. "There are bruises that look like someone's fingers on his arm. Someone tried to hurt him."

Now there's total silence. Everyone knows that by "someone" Steph means one of the aides. When something like this happens, it's always aides against nurses.

I know for certain that Jenna would never hurt Jeff, but I can't say the same about every single one of the other aides. I've never seen them do anything cruel, just thoughtless and maybe a little bit mean sometimes. But if Jeff infuriated someone, because he hurt them by accident, I'm not sure what would happen.

I know it's unfair, but in my mind it's one of the guys who did this. Just not sure which one.

I look out from the conference room. Right now, Ben is helping Thomas with physical therapy, Jeremy is feeding Louise, and that weird new guy is off in the corner changing someone's diaper. I can't see who it is from here even when I crane my neck.

My money is on the weird new guy, but of course I can't say anything. I don't know him at all.

"Let's talk about next steps," Steph says. "I want you all to be extra vigilant for the next few weeks, until we find out who's responsible for this. If anyone has any information at all, I need to know. Yesterday."

Silence while we all absorb this. No one wants to be the person who turns someone else in.

But if someone hurt Jeff, it's possible they might hurt Gulie next. Or Thomas. Or Louise. Or Mandy who thinks it's hilarious to watch from her wheelchair until someone comes close by and then grab onto them and not let go.

Yeah, Mandy can be very irritating. She might be next.

I try to tell myself that the other children, except for Mandy, aren't as annoying as Jeff. But I don't know what started all this. What set someone off so that they did the unthinkable act of hurting a child despite all their training and experience?

I also know, despite the strong feeling in the room, that it might not be an aide who's responsible. It might be a nurse.

I tell myself that we only have four male nurses right now, but then I realize it might be a woman. Surely that's less likely, but still.

If it turns out that I have to report someone, my loyalty will be to the children, not to the staff.

"Are there any questions?" Steph asks. "If not, let's get back to work, people."

No questions, just a sense of desolation. No one makes eye contact.

And now what? I go behind the nurse's station to start on morning meds. Gulie careens into my leg. She's on her way somewhere, but only she knows where she is going.

I stroke Gulie's hair before pointing her in the direction of the playroom. I smile at the aides out of habit (it would be wrong to ignore them, wouldn't it? Everyone is innocent until proven guilty).

Now Steph calls the aides to the conference room. We

pretend not to watch the shock on their faces as she tells them about Jeff. The mood is low already but feels like Beebe's bathysphere at the bottom of the ocean when the aides come back into the playroom.

I pretend I can't talk to anyone. I'm concentrating on crushing the meds, mixing them with applesauce to help the kids swallow.

But Jenna comes over to me. I can't ignore her. "How could this happen?" she says, in real pain. "Do you know who it is?"

"I don't." I look at her sideways; after all, she is an aide, she may know more than I do. "Do you know who it is?"

She glares at me. "Of course not. I would tell Steph if I did."

I have a bad feeling that it will take weeks, if not months, to solve this mystery. For that entire time, the children will be in danger. If I could watch over them twenty-four hours a day, I would...but I can't. Even I know this.

The outside doors open, and some emergency medical technicians bring Jeff back into the playroom. He is strapped to a gurney and doesn't like it. His left arm is in a sky-blue cast, and he is howling, gigantic tears falling out of his eyes so fast his shirt is soaking wet.

Jeff's not doing it on purpose, but if you don't know him, you might think he's trying to hurt someone. His arms flail, and his legs kick the technicians. He even pinches them with his good hand.

Ordinarily the aides would rush over to reclaim Jeff, but now they are afraid to touch him.

I lock up my med cart and help free Jeff so he can crawl around the playroom, and slowly his sobbing stops. He sits by himself, unable to tell us what happened.

I started this day in a ruined castle, and now it will end in one.

Chapter Twelve

And I would also be ready for the hospital, for vile odors and trying sights. –Peri Klass, *Other Women's Children*

Before the next emergency tonight, I will travel to Vienna.

There are so many reasons to go there, leaving aside the full moon craziness in the hospital tonight. I've always wanted to see Lipizzaner horses perform at the Spanish Riding School. They are trained how to dance, in what is known as airs above the ground. I can't imagine anything more unearthly. Most of these white horses have dark eyes and some have dark noses that I long to pet. It would be like petting a unicorn.

If I am really lucky, I might see the horses outside in the Burggarten. I might go there to drink Viennese coffee and eat a Viennese pastry that tastes of cinnamon and chocolate. To be nice to my brother, I'll take a picture of the statue of Mozart and send it to him. After all, the statue won't be playing music.

I also want to visit the Schmetterlinghaus, where butterflies wander safely out of the reach of predators. I think every living being should have a Schmetterlinghaus.

I don't have to stop there. As a savvy traveller, I buy a Vienna PASS so I can access public transportation. The buses are bright yellow, like American school buses full of tourists instead of children. I might look like a tourist to everyone else, but I know I'm different.

I'll skip the Giant Ferris Wheel but spend some time at the Kunsthistorisches Museum to admire The Hunters in the Snow by Pieter Bruegel. I have a reproduction of this painting in my apartment. I love the colors, and how Bruegel paints animals. Seeing the real painting will be overwhelming.

Then I'll hop off at the Schönbrunn Zoo. Any place with an umlaut sounds good to me. This one has not only a Panorama train, but also a bat cave (a real one, not a Batman and Robin one).

This is what Seneca meant when he said, "Travel and change of place impart new vigor to the mind." But Seneca lived in Roman times, so his travels were limited to Corsica and southern Italy. Too bad. I bet he would be an excellent travel companion to take all over Europe. Not too talkative. A Stoic about trains that don't arrive on time.

But now I am called to a different floor to help with a patient who's having a baby. And all my newfound vigor goes out the window.

Most of our floors are converted into COVID-19 inpatient units. But there is still one place where mothers come to give birth. Getting admitted to a hospital used to be straightforward. Now, it's harder than getting into heaven.

There are tests. First, outside the hospital, an aide comes running with a wheelchair. Even if the mother is bent over with contractions and screaming bloody murder, she needs to answer a series of questions about potential viral symptoms. The aide records her answers, hoping she's telling the truth. Then takes her temperature to see if it's possible she has the virus but is in denial or doesn't know it.

If her temperature is normal, the aide performs a rapid antigen test, and we pray it's not a false negative. If the test is positive, whoever is pushing the wheelchair turns around and takes the patient to a different floor, because that's a whole different kind of birth.

Usually, by the time we see results on the test (nothing is rapid if you're having contractions) the mother is ready to kill us. Whether or not she's allowed into the maternity floor.

The aide puts a makeshift ID bracelet on the mother. And then we have to tell her that her partner, the one she's been counting on to get her through labor, can't come inside. Even though we apologize and assure her we will be with her through the entire process, this news is never received well. As in, the mother uses the most colorful four-letter word language she can think of. I don't blame her one bit.

The partner is usually unhappy about this, too. Husband or mother or friend, it really doesn't matter. Some kind gentle person has to reassure the partner and get them to leave, which also generates a lot of foul language.

To enter this floor, I have to change my paper gown, gloves, mask and shoe covers to avoid contamination. There's a special room staffed with volunteers to help during the day. Not at night, of course. It's as if they're ignoring the fact that most labor starts at night and ends early in the morning before it gets light. I struggle through this involved process alone. I'm a perfectionist, so it takes me awhile. I know other nurses are waiting for me, but I can't take the risk of bringing bacteria or, worse yet, virus onto this floor.

Then I use my key card to go through an airlock designed to let in or let out one person at a time.

In the best of all possible nursing worlds, I stay on the same floor where I am originally assigned all night. But I'm being called on to this floor because one of the nurses started vomiting and had to go home in the middle of the night.

Most nurses love this kind of assignment. I hate it. I hate being around mothers and babies. It's not just too much history. With every birth, I worry that something new will go wrong, something I don't know how to handle.

What if these mothers knew that nine months after they had sex, they'd have to give birth during a pandemic? I bet every single one would say, "I'll skip the sex, thank you. It's just not worth it."

But they didn't know. And now it's too late.

Tonight's victim is a young woman having her first baby. She's scared and miserable without her husband. It doesn't help that her doctor hasn't arrived yet. I don't know Maude, the nurse assigned to this floor, very well as I hardly ever float here. She's young and competent and confident in a way I never was. She's trying to make the patient comfortable, but it's not working out so well.

I forget that the patient can't see me smiling at her when I introduce myself and ask her name (Wilma. Really?).

I can't see if she looks slightly more relaxed because she's wearing a mask, too. I don't remember much about giving birth to Sara, but I do remember yelling. If someone told me I had to wear a mask, I might have crammed it down their throat. But I'm going to encourage this woman to yell and curse and let it all out behind her mask.

It turns out Wilma is the Stoic type too, or maybe she's used to not making a fuss and repressing her pain, like most women.

I give her ice chips to chew on. I let her squeeze my (gloved) hand during contractions. I can tell how much pain she's in from how hard she squeezes. I gently massage her shoulders which are as stiff as a sword. Although Wilma doesn't say much, she communicates apprehension with her eyes.

Finally, her doctor waltzes in, masked but somehow gleaming and smelling of aftershave. Immediately Wilma's attention shifts from us to him. I can tell she's smiling with relief and hero worship behind her mask.

Now we're all working as a team, with the doctor in position to catch the baby. I'm the cheerleader telling Wilma how great she's doing as the doctor decides when she needs to push and when she needs to hold back.

So much positivity. Keep going, Wilma, you're almost through, rah rah rah, it's going to be worth every second, blah blah blah, every cliché I can dish out. I don't think she believes me, but she nods and grunts and follows instructions.

And then everyone smiles because the head is out safely, and now the rest of the baby slides through. A big, fat, healthy boy.

Even I smile. The baby's head swivels on his adorably creased neck. The room is brightly lit and cold. All the baby sees are unfamiliar masked faces. Of course, he'd rather return to the nice warm dark comfortable womb where he spent nine months growing.

Now the baby is screaming that he wants to go back where he came from. That's just what we want to hear.

"Have you picked out a name, Wilma?" Maude asks. Always the same questions. We do the same things we always do. Record the Apgar scores (today, these are fine). Wipe off the blood and vernix, wrap the baby in a blanket, hand him to the mother.

I'm glad I don't usually work this floor; it's got to be boring after a while. All this happiness.

"His name is Benjamin," Wilma answers as she holds the baby. "Can I call my husband and tell him?"

Maude helps Wilma with her cell phone while I jiggle fussy Benjamin and walk him around the room. He looks perfectly healthy, but he's a bruiser with wide shoulders, weighing eight pounds ten ounces. He might have fractured a clavicle on his way through the birth canal. It's too early to tell. If something like that is wrong, hopefully the pediatrician will catch it on Ben's first visit.

That's the thing about babies—you have to wait to see how they come out. I don't like surprises.

"He's so cute!" Maude gushes. She's standing beside me

eating the baby with her eyes instead of her mouth.

"And big, and hungry," I agree. "Let's see if he wants to breastfeed."

We give Wilma and Benjamin their first lesson in the art of nursing, but Benjamin has no trouble latching on. It's good he's not a twin, because he's not leaving a drop of milk for anyone else. Wilma looks blissful.

And just for a moment, I forget that this is a pandemic and even when something good happens, something terrible can happen in the next second. I'm caught up in Wilma's delight and Benjamin's satisfaction.

Just for a moment, I have no need to travel back to the Burggarten, because everything I need is here.

Chapter Thirteen

There is nothing so expensive, really, as a big, well-developed, full-bodied preconception.
–E.B. White, *One Man's Meat*

About three months ago, after Yonatan leaves, I think I should consider becoming a nurse practitioner so I can prescribe drugs and be all powerful. Maybe seek a position at a different hospital.

I go to a nursing conference in Delaware to learn more about the courses needed to get an advanced degree. All I know about Delaware is they do a lot of car racing there, and in Georgetown, Delaware, you can admire the world's largest frying pan. Fried food does not appeal to me.

But I am wrong about not liking this state. I take Amtrak to the conference in Wilmington, Delaware. I have a window seat, and nobody asks to sit next to me (I would move my bag if necessary, but in the middle of a pandemic, hardly any trains are running, and fewer people are riding them).

From the window, I see more egrets and herons than I've ever seen before! They don't seem afraid of the train at all; they don't even look up when the train goes by. The birds are left in peace, not surrounded by acquisitive people who want to take over their habitat to use for expensive houses.

So far, Delaware seems like a good place to work, maybe even a good place to live and work. Maybe better than Pennsylvania. At least for birds.

Not sure about how good it is for people, though. At least, not yet.

The meeting takes place at the Chase Center on the Riverfront. It's fine. I mean, it isn't as good as the train, but the building is new and modern, industrial style, I guess. It is an easy place to be invisible. And therefore safe.

I listen to teachers extol the virtues of their program and collect lots of literature. Then I go outside and walk around looking for a restaurant that isn't too crowded. Because I don't like people to notice when I eat alone. Or to see that I don't eat fried food. And I read while I eat.

The best part is, I find a bookstore to hide in until I have to catch my next train. A black man is doing a poetry reading there, and I like the sound of his voice.

I buy his book afterwards. I'll read it on the train. Then I walk around the market area until it is time for me to go home.

I never do follow up on that program, but I still have all the literature, and the book signed by the author.

So now, when I feel stressed, I think about all those birds living in Delaware away from the dirty water of the cities.

There must be fresh fish in the waterways or how could they survive?

I'm stressed today. When I go to put on my scrubs to get ready for work, the bottoms look like clown pants after I tie them on.

I haven't been eating much because I'm so worried about Jeff at the Center. And I work there today. I'll have to see if I can find smaller scrubs in the laundry room, because wearing this pair is just mortifying.

I used to enjoy walking into the Center and saying hello to everyone. I feel at home there. But now, I duck my head when I see other staff. I have no idea who is guilty.

Is it someone I never liked? Someone I won't mind turning in? Or someone I thought of as a friend?

At least I can look at the children in the playroom. They're innocent.

Jeff is still wearing his cast, but he seems to feel better. He's learned to scoot around without putting weight on his bad arm. He's playing with some plastic dinosaurs, chewing on them and throwing them across the room with his good arm.

Gulie is sitting leaning against the wall, her eyes partially closed. It's unusual for her to remain this still. I'll have to check night notes to see if she had trouble sleeping.

Mandy and Thomas and Louise are in their wheelchairs in front of the gigantic TV. Only Louise appears to be watching Odd Squad. I'm not sure why it's on instead of a cartoon; I think the math is too hard for the kids to follow. Mandy is more interested in bobbing her head up and down. Thomas has fallen sideways in his chair.

I straighten him up and whisper "Hi, Thomas," because I don't want to disturb Louise by talking too loudly. I get a radiant smile from Thomas. The aide who's supposed to be taking care of Thomas doesn't look up from his phone. It's the weird new guy. One more reason not to like him too much.

Before the pandemic, on weekends, the aides used to take the children in wheelchairs on field trips to museums and libraries and even puppet shows. But now the TV has become their main source of entertainment. I understand why it's happening, but I don't think it's a good idea.

"Do you think you could get some crayons out?" I say to the new guy sharply. "Or maybe fingerpaints? If you're too tired to take Thomas outside, that is." It's a nice day, so why keep everyone inside?

The new guy kind of jerks and looks nervous. But he gets up and goes to the art closet. He finds a roll of shelf paper and some crayons, the oversized ones that are easier for Thomas to use.

He wheels Thomas to an empty table and helps him grasp a crayon so he can make random scribbles on the paper.

Thomas smiles.

The new guy sits next to him at the table so he can give Thomas new crayon colors when it looks as if he's stopped drawing. He's not ungentle, just thoughtless.

"That's better," I approve. "What's your name, anyway?"

The new guy looks horrified. "Uh, Martin."

"We haven't been formally introduced, Martin. I'm Sonia."

He nods.

"I know you're new here, so if you have any questions, I'd

be happy to answer them."

He looks away.

Well, I have some questions for you, Martin. Why are you here? Do you even like children? Are you cruel to any of them? Did you break Jeff's arm?

Gulie is on her feet and is starting her usual rounds. She smells as if she needs a diaper change. I take her behind the nurse's station and clean her up. She pulls my hair and cries a little, but then takes off to run around the room, slapping herself and smiling as usual.

While I prepare morning meds, I let myself think about Yonatan.

What was the point of Yonatan, anyway?

Before I meet Yonatan, I think a lot about returning to Peter and Sara. After I meet him, I sever my relationship with them. At least, mentally.

My relationship with my parent is already over. Which is maybe the whole point of my leaving, anyway. Or maybe not. I don't like to think about it too much. So, I don't.

After I tell my parents I am leaving my marriage, they stop speaking to me. I think they tell my brother, but he doesn't have any children, so he doesn't care. I mean, we never speak, so I don't think anything I do matters to him anyway.

I think his wife knows though. She calls me sometimes to let me know how my brother is doing since his heart attack. Sometimes she gets a little vague while she's talking to me, her tempo is a little off. As if she wants to say something but doesn't have the guts.

I mean, how good is their marriage, after all? Good enough

to criticize me? I don't think so.

Still, I don't have a good reason to fall in love with Yonatan. He comes to the Center when I am vulnerable. Lonely. Feeling as if it might be a mistake to leave one box only to get stuck in another.

That's not a good reason to fall in love. At least, not if love is supposed to be rational. But who says it is?

I love the children at the Center, but I still miss Peter and Sara, if I'm being honest with myself. I love my cat, and my tiny apartment, but sometimes I wish I never left my former life. Not very often, but still.

The way things are going, the way I feel, I might write to Peter. I might ask for pictures of Sara.

Then Yonatan comes and for a few months, there is excitement, and anticipation, and conversation.

Instead of being stuck in a box, I feel I am living on a whole new planet where I am special instead of ordinary. I am special because Yonatan sees me, the real me.

That's why sharing knowledge with Yonatan, teaching him English, gives me joy. And then it becomes so hard not to kiss him. It is a relief when he kisses me. Even though I walk away at first.

Working together means keeping a wondrous secret from everyone else at the Center. Except I think Louise knows. She pinches me a lot during that time. But I don't care.

If we work during the day, we always leave in separate cars so no one will guess our secret. But at night, even though I leave the Center fifteen minutes after Yonatan, he waits for me in the parking lot so I can get into his red Volkswagen.

For a few hours, we can be together in the dark.

I hide my car in the library parking lot on those nights because no one ever goes there. I think I'm the only one who takes out books instead of ordering them from Amazon. In this whole town.

Well, maybe one or two students go there, too. But they don't ever come to the Center.

That kind of happiness drives away all thought of consequences. Of right and wrong. Of Peter and Sara. There's only the happiness of each moment with someone you love.

I have it. And then I lose it when Yonatan leaves.

Since then, I wonder if I should try to get it back again. Maybe become a nurse practitioner and move to the same city where Yonatan is now.

But then I will lose the children at the Center. Of course, I might lose them, or some of them, to the virus anyway. But now I feel I can't leave them until the pandemic is over. If it ever ends. If the world ever goes back to normal.

Anyway, I don't think Yonatan is like Peter, still waiting for me to come home.

How do I know Peter is waiting? I just know.

Yonatan is not the sort of man who does well alone, without admiration and without someone to make a home for him and take care of him. Is he looking for someone else? Has he found them by now? Probably.

It seems as if I'm being asked to give something up. My life, for Peter and Sara. The children at the Center, for Yonatan.

I can pretend to be noble and say I give up Peter and Sara

for the children. But I can't pretend anything if I go to live in Delaware with Yonatan.

And maybe not with Yonatan, because why should he come back to me if he finds someone else and is happy?

Yonatan gives me joy, but I think he is more grateful to me than in love with me.

Peter gives me Sara, but any joy we have disappears too quickly.

I don't know if I can ever get that joy back. If we can get it back.

If the pandemic ever ends.

Part Two: Peter

Chapter Fourteen

She read books as one would breathe air, to fill up and live.
–Annie Dillard, *The Living*

When we are first married, one night, sitting in front of the fireplace, Sonia tells me about her gift of travelling.

Her long hair is braided down her back, and the firelight illuminates wayward tendrils that escape and curl around her face. She keeps pushing them back as if they interfere with her story.

I love Sonia's hair, the length of it, how soft it is, and how the gentle light brown color is interspersed with sun-colored strands.

She tells me how, as a child, her brother won all the awards at school and was her father's favorite because he was a musical prodigy.

"Why was that so important to you?" I ask. "Why did you want your father's approval so badly?"

Sonia looks at me as if suddenly, I have turned into a Republican.

"Doesn't everyone want their parents' approval? Isn't that normal?"

I shrug. "I want my parents to be proud of me, sure. But I don't live to make them happy."

I can tell from the way Sonia looks at me that she doesn't believe this.

I elaborate.

"I wouldn't change anything about who I am, and what I want out of life for my parents. I expect them to go along with my ideas because they raised me to question their authority."

"But you're a doctor," Sonia says accusingly. "How could anyone not be proud of a son who's a doctor?"

"Well, my dad is an architect, and my mom is a sculptor. I think they hoped I'd be some kind of artist. I just didn't have that kind of talent. But they didn't hold it against me."

Sonia looks skeptical.

"Weren't your parents proud of you when you became a nurse?" I ask.

Sonia shakes her head. "When I became a nurse," she says, "It was just a job. Like being a secretary. I still wasn't my brother."

She doesn't say anymore, but she doesn't need to. I understand where she got this idea of travelling. She invented something her brother can never do.

I just don't understand why she still needs to travel. Away from us. Now that she's got me and Sara.

And why she's been away so long.

You might think I'm crazy because I'm not crazy worried. The way I see it, the whole essence of travelling is that you go there, and then you come back.

This could still happen. Sonia could return.

At any minute.

When Sonia used to research all those trips on her computer, she would take notes and tell me about those places after dinner.

I guess I should have paid more attention at the time. Because at some point, she stops telling me all the details.

It is just that…

I think I have more important things to worry about. Like making the house welcoming, because Sonia doesn't seem to want to do that.

And, after Sara comes, being a partner to Sonia in taking care of our baby.

And normal things like my job. Or playing tennis with my friends so they don't think I deserted them just because I am married and have a baby.

Also, I guess I am wrong, but I think we are still happy.

Until we aren't. Because Sonia is gone.

I come home one night to find the house empty.

I don't panic at first because Sonia sends me a text earlier that day saying she is going for a long hike. She leaves Sara with our neighbors.

This doesn't happen very often, but occasionally, our neighbors agree to babysit. They have a little boy close to Sara's age. The kids are too little to do much except roll around on the floor together.

So, the first thing I do is go over to Jan and Ted's house to collect Sara. I thank them and offer to watch their boy one afternoon if they want to go out.

Jan thanks me and says how much she will enjoy an afternoon off. She will be in touch.

When I look back at that night, it is all very calm and civilized. As if we are characters in a movie. No one says anything that makes me think Sonia is acting differently than usual.

I take Sara home and change her and put her in her highchair with some toys to keep her busy while I warm up her dinner. I think Sonia will be home before we start eating.

But she isn't.

I send her a text asking where she is and get no response. That's weird, but I'm still not worried. I'm too busy.

I spend an hour trying to get Sara to eat some pureed vegetables instead of finger painting with them. Afterwards we both need a bath.

Then I put Sara to bed (read a story, sing a song, say good night, repeat as needed) and go into my office. I try to call Sonia. No answer.

That's when I find a very long note from Sonia left on my computer desk.

She tells me to take good care of Sara. This part of the note is extremely detailed.

After giving me paragraph after paragraph of step-by-step instructions for keeping Sara happy, Sonia writes she is going away for a while to a place where she will be safe.

She doesn't want me to worry about her. Or try to find her.

Just to trust her.

I don't know if I can.

But Sonia doesn't sound as if she is out of her mind.

Or the least bit suicidal.

I don't know what will happen if I don't listen to her. Maybe she will never come back.

If I do exactly what she asks, maybe she will come back.

I wait.

It's sort of okay at first. Sara is too young to understand what's going on. I try to act normal around her, so I don't frighten her or make her feel sad.

I stay home from work for a few days, saying my back is out.

I interview woman after woman until I find a nanny I can trust. I don't know what I'm thinking, exactly, but I go to a very expensive and highly recommended agency to find a live-in nanny who is bilingual in English and Italian.

Most of the women they send are so young, I don't trust them with Sara.

The nanny I pick is old and strict, and she has a mustache. She does not exactly speak English well. Close enough, though. Her name is Alessia

She tells me haltingly that she is visiting her grandson, who works at Genentech, but the pandemic interrupts her time with family. Now she cannot return to Italy for a while and needs a job to stay here.

I sign all the paperwork necessary for an extended work visa.

I offer Alessia our best guest room and a tremendous

amount of money per week because when I hand Sara over to her, she accepts her with complete authority.

I can tell Sara loves her already.

I have some vague idea that it will be educational for Sara to hear another language while her mother is away. And maybe I can study Italian too, and someday when Sonia returns, we will visit Rome together and go to all the museums.

I don't want Sonia to think that Sara and I just sit around feeling sad while she is gone.

Instead, we are working on our Italian and planning to travel. We are improving ourselves.

Won't that make Sonia want to come home? Won't she contact us soon to ask how we are doing? And tell us she's coming home?

Except she never does. And that makes me so angry.

But I keep telling myself there is a reason for it.

Now that no one can travel and everything is closed and almost everyone is working from home, the thought of travelling seems almost funny. A luxury that no one can take seriously.

We have money, so we manage.

Alessia wakes up early and goes to sleep late. She is here even on weekends when she is supposed to take both days off. She keeps the door of her room shut all the time, even when she is downstairs taking care of Sara. I would not dream of going in there.

Sometimes I hear her talking on her cellphone late at night. I want to ask her about her family in Italy, but I'm afraid I'll hear something I'll never be able to forget.

I offer her the use of my car on weekends, but she looks forbidding and shakes her head no. She wears a mask all the time, whether she is indoors or not.

Sara doesn't seem to notice except when Alessia picks her up, she tries to take the mask off her face and Alessia tells her "Lascia stare la mia maschera, piccola." Sara and I are both learning Italian.

We order our groceries online and they are delivered to our house without me ever seeing who leaves them outside. It's called "contactless service."

And that's what my world feels like right now. I've lost my contact with Sonia.

And now, all contact is dangerous.

I try to work at home as much as I can. As a radiologist, I rarely need to make actual appearances at the hospital. X-rays are supremely portable. I read them on my home computer, and send my comments back without ever talking to anyone.

Working at home is the best way to keep my family safe. And also to keep myself sane.

Because it feels as if the world could end at any moment. If it does, I want to be here with my daughter.

Of course, I wonder what's happening with Sonia. Is she being careful? Does she ever think about me? About Sara? I feel she does.

I don't think Sonia can be travelling anymore. If that's what she did when she left us.

And if she's not travelling, maybe she's thinking about coming back.

Unless…

Maybe living here with us was like reading a book for Sonia. Not a real part of her life, just an interlude.

Sonia is one of the fastest readers I ever met. If she went on a train ride, she would carry two books, not one, because she was afraid of finishing too soon. So she is used to books ending earlier than she wants them to.

Chapter Fifteen

There are some things you learn best in calm, and some in storm. –Willa Cather, *The Song of the Lark*

When Sara is born, I order a video camera from Best Buy. I'm not one of those creepy husbands who take pictures of their wives giving birth, screaming and wild-eyed in labor. Not that Sonia is like that. She tries to hide all her pain.

During contractions, she squeezes my hand hard, very hard. No recriminations. Just concentration on bringing Sara into this world.

I buy the video camera to record Sara's milestones. When she nurses. When she smiles. When she turns over.

I ask Sonia to record these for me if I am at work and miss them. I show her how to use the camera. It's easy. I promise to do the same for her.

If Sara has a breakthrough accomplishment and Sonia is out shopping or if she decides to go back to work, neither of us miss any of these unrepeatable moments.

But Sonia doesn't see any reason to make a record of Sara's achievements. I guess her parents never did this for her.

She refuses to use the camera. When I take it with us on picnics or trips to the playground, Sonia never wants to be in the videos.

"I don't photograph well," is her excuse. "Take all the pictures you want of Sara. But don't ever point that thing at me."

Sara stars in those early videos. If you didn't know better, you'd think she didn't have a mother. Although Sonia is right there the whole time.

Sometimes you can hear her voice in the background. But most of the time, she's invisible.

My childhood is different. I've seen so many movies of myself walking, grinning, playing with a ball, finger painting. My parents love to get these videos out at every birthday, to show me how far I've come.

I want Sara to have that same sense of family. Even if right now, I'm not sure what family means. Are you still family if you leave? How did Gauguin's family feel about him after his departure?

I think of Sonia probably squeezed into a small apartment since she left. Then I think of all the people who live in small apartments out of necessity.

I feel for them these past few months. Being shut inside a tiny place, not knowing when it's safe to go out. Nothing to do but watch TV. Hoping that when you go to the pharmacy or the store, you're not bringing virus back with you.

At first, being stuck at home seems like a vacation, but it gets boring fast. Children feel bewildered to have their boundaries tightened for so long. I'm glad Sara is a baby and doesn't know what she's missing. The outside world. Her mother.

We're lucky to have this big house and big yard. I have exercise equipment in the basement. I try to use it every day because our gym is closed, indefinitely.

I doubt the gym will suspend payment during the pandemic for the months we can't take advantage of our incredibly expensive family membership. These new scary rules are hard on gym owners, too.

I used to enjoy going to the gym. I looked forward to swimming in their Olympic-sized pool. Sometimes I used the sauna afterwards. Now I have to force myself to use the boring stationary bike and treadmill in the basement instead.

Our backyard is landscaped for minimal upkeep. I have automatic sprinklers and gravel instead of grass, and a tall fence protected by security cameras.

It doesn't look pretty, exactly, more like an armed fortress.

I know I can't keep virus out, but I'm grateful we pick this big house with all this privileged space outside. Even though Sonia protests when we buy the house and wants something much smaller.

If Sonia returns tomorrow, she will feel differently. Won't she?

She will be thankful we have a way to separate ourselves from the terror of the virus.

Currently, we're safe in here—I hope—all by ourselves.

Our fractured family. Sara, Alessia and I.

I spend a fortune installing safety surfacing under ambitious recreational equipment designed to help make Sara athletic and independent as she grows up. She's too young to appreciate it yet.

But now that we can't go to the playground or the park, I take Sara out in the backyard and photograph her on the baby swing. I push the swing hard so I can get the image of Sara swooping through the air, laughing and waving her arms.

Sara knows she's safe when I push her. She never tries to hold onto the handlebars. Of course, I never forget to buckle her in, even when she struggles.

See, Sonia? Here is your daughter, already taller than when you left, and stronger. You're missing so much.

The one good part about this godawful pandemic is that at least I get to spend more time with Sara. I wonder if this will make a difference to our relationship as she grows older. Maybe she'll turn into a daddy's girl and follow me around everywhere.

I will love that.

Currently, though, Sara doesn't do much except smile when she sees me.

Of course, she smiles when she sees Alessia, too. She reaches out her little arms to Alessia as I hand her over.

I wonder if her brain is absorbing the Italian spirito del tempo of constantly mopping and dusting as Alessia carries Sara around the house.

Alessia only takes Sara outside if I insist. Mostly, they stay in the kitchen after Alessia cleans the house every day.

She scowls and yells at me in Italian when I tell her cleaning is not part of her job.

Our housekeeper doesn't come anymore because of the virus, but I don't need her.

Alessia is teaching Sara how to bake fresh bread every day. She lets her punch down the dough, which is a lot of sticky fun for a baby.

Alessia doesn't treat Sara like a baby. More like a tiny adult. I wonder how much Sara will remember of all these cooking lessons when she gets older.

I order less and less butter from our grocery store. If I forget and put some on the table, Alessia takes it away and replaces it with a small bowl of olive oil.

If any bread is left over, Alessia puts it outside for the birds. I try to tell her that breadcrumbs may not be good for birds, but my Italian isn't up to it yet. I know Alessia speaks English—I interviewed her for this job in English, for God's sake—but lately, when I speak to her in English, she pretends not to understand.

Alessia teaches Sara to cook a lot of vegetable dishes that I've never heard of. Not as much pasta as you'd think. But when the two of them do cook pasta, it's delicious. I think Alessia makes it by hand.

I hope Sara remembers or absorbs at least some of how to do this.

When she puts Sara down for a nap, Alessia sings her a song with the words "Stella Stellina" in it. There are other words I don't understand yet, but the song really works to put Sara to sleep.

I should learn this song so I can sing it to Sara after Sonia comes home and Alessia goes back to Italy. I need to work harder on my Italian. If I don't learn this song, Sara may never sleep again after Alessia is gone. It will happen someday, and I won't be prepared.

Alessia takes the baby Cam with her and works in the garden she has started in the backyard until Sara wakes up from her nap.

I give Alessia some memory foam mats because I catch her kneeling in the dirt, wearing pantyhose and her black dress and apron. I've never seen Alessia wear any other clothes.

I don't know where she gets the seeds for the vegetables she's growing. Maybe she orders them from Amazon.

The vegetables are already coming up. There are rabbits in the garden. I don't know how they get in, but they make our fancy fence look like a complete waste of money.

Sara squeals and laughs when she sees the rabbits hopping around, so I don't do anything to try to keep them out. I don't know what to do, anyway.

I think Alessia tells the rabbits not to eat the vegetables, or she'll eat the rabbits.

Maybe Alessia is a witch. A good one. If they have those in Italy.

She seems like someone from a fairy tale, anyway.

I try to get to Sara first after naptime. Sometimes she has a hard wakeup, and I think I'm more sympathetic than Alessia when Sara cries.

It's always hard to hand Sara over to Alessia by the time Alessia gets up the stairs. There's a part of me that wants to put Sara into her car seat and drive away until we find Sonia and bring her home.

But I can't do that now because of the virus.

I should be grateful that Sara and I have a place to live that is relatively safe and most of the time, I can work from home.

I should be grateful that the three of us are not sick. Or hospitalized. Or dead.

All right, I am grateful. But I'm not happy.

I can't say I'm lonely because I have Sara. Taking care of a baby is like having a gigantic pillow protecting you from everything that's horrible in the world.

But I miss Sonia and our life together. Working at home by myself feels like a punishment instead of a vacation.

Sara can't protect me from missing her mother. And I have no idea what Alessia thinks about Sonia being gone so long. She never says a word to me about it.

When I hire Alessia, I say that her mother will be away for a while, and Alessia just nods. Is it a little weird that she's never asked me a question about Sonia since then?

I wonder. If I worked out a way to stay home and pay more attention to Sonia and Sara, would Sonia have left? Is this all my fault?

Or is Sonia's travelling inevitable? Something that has nothing to do with me?

It's not as if I tried to keep her at home. I wanted her to travel around the world with me. She seemed to enjoy it at first. Until she didn't.

I still don't know what happened inside Sonia to make her leave us. And maybe I won't ever know. But I can't forget about it and move on. I'm stuck until she comes back.

If I was a character in a cartoon, I would sit down on a bench and find someone had put glue on it and my pants were stuck to it. I'm so stuck on Sonia, I would starve to death.

Of course, this is real life. I can be angry. I can move.

I just can't get anywhere without Sonia.

At dinner, I take the food out to the picnic table in the backyard. I bring Sara's highchair out so she can watch the rabbits. It's easier to spoon food into Sara's mouth while she's distracted and happy.

Alessia doesn't look as if she's enjoying herself, but she doesn't argue about it.

She's good about putting suntan lotion on Sara before we leave the house. When Sara fusses, she talks to her in Italian, and the fussing stops. I'm just as glad I don't know what Alessia is saying.

Tonight, the light is good. I bring out the video camera and make a movie of Sara waving at the rabbits. Later, after I'm sure she's digested her dinner, I put her in the swing and ask Alessia to push her so I can immortalize Sara flying through the sky.

I don't take any video of Alessia. Just of Sara.

I want Sara to look back someday and see how happy she was as a baby.

Even though her mother isn't in the video.

Chapter Sixteen

She was one of those who are born to make chaos cosmic. –Max Beerbohm, *Zuleika Dobson*

I
f death disappears, I might like the pandemic a little bit.

No flights. No trains. No traffic jams.

The world is in reset mode. A moment of stillness.

No.

A moment of stillness is a respite. Not months of it.

This is an ice age. Everyone is dying and no one knows when it will end.

I've stopped expecting Sonia to walk in the door. Even if she wants to travel home, I know she can't go anywhere.

And that makes me worry about Sonia feeling alone out there. Even if it's her choice. Or was her choice. What if she's changed her mind and now it's too late to do anything about it?

In some ways, this separation from people feels like the end of the world. I don't know what I would do if I didn't have Sara to take my mind off the pandemic.

And Alessia, of course, to take care of Sara.

I exercise very hard in the basement between four and five in the morning. I wake up thinking Sonia is here. I reach for her across the pillow. But I can't touch her hair. And then I remember.

So, I go down to the basement and run way too fast on the treadmill during these early hours when everyone else is sleeping and no one expects me to be productive.

I'm not going anywhere, but it makes me feel as if I have a way out. If I don't run, I'll want to throw things, glass things that shatter with a satisfying crunch. And that will frighten Sara.

Also, Alessia will have to clean up the mess. I don't want to make more work for her.

Then.

Slowly.

Slowly.

What seems impossible the day before the pandemic starts begins to feel normal.

I become accustomed to this incredibly small world of the three of us. Hating it. But accepting it. What choice do I have?

Months pass without holidays. Sara is too young to miss chocolates on Easter or fireworks on July Fourth. I don't feel like celebrating by ourselves, anyway.

Celebration means Sonia to me.

Then, one morning while I'm feeding Sara breakfast, and Alessia is folding laundry, all three of us are startled when the doorbell rings.

No, we are not expecting anyone. Not even a grocery delivery today.

Maybe it's a lost Amazon driver. They still leave packages full of baby toys for Sara, books for me.

I'd order something for Alessia if I knew what she would like, but I have no clue.

When I look at my doorbell app, I drop the phone on the floor from shock.

Sonia's parents are at the door.

I grab my phone and run over to open it. They're wearing sunglasses and masks, but I'm not.

"Just a minute," I yell. I need time to unwrap a mask from the container by the door.

"Peter, it's Olivia and Terence," Sonia's mother calls from outside.

"I'm coming!" I've got my mask on now. I go outside the house and stand by the door, motioning them to back up.

Olivia and Terence eyes register confusion, but they back down the steps until we're easily six feet apart.

Everyone is used to social distancing by now. It's become second nature after months of no physical contact.

Especially no hugging. Even with relatives you haven't seen and didn't expect to see until the pandemic ends.

Even if…

"Is this an emergency?" I ask. "Has something happened to Sonia?"

"No, no." Olivia turns to face me, holding herself back from touching my arm. "We haven't heard from Sonia since she left."

"We haven't heard from you, at all," Terence adds. "That's why we're here."

Oliva is a small, slender woman wearing thick glasses. Terence is bigger and burlier. It's hard to tell what they're thinking without seeing their faces under their masks. Their clothes look creased and worn. They must have travelled a long way to get here.

Although I met Sonia's parents before our wedding, they seem like strangers.

They look past me, as if they're trying to use x-ray vision to find Sara inside the house. I look too, but Alessia has taken Sara out of her highchair, and I can't see anyone from out here on the porch.

"We thought it was about time to talk," Olivia says. "And meet our grand daughter."

"How did you get here?" I ask. "No one's supposed to travel right now."

They rent a small house in Douglas, Arizona. It's close enough to drive to visit their son in New Mexico. but not close to their daughter.

They've never come to our house before. Partly because it's so far away, but also because Sonia never invited them.

"We drove," Terence said. "We packed all our food and slept in the trailer to avoid exposure. We were very careful."

"We made good time," Olivia adds. "There aren't a lot of cars on the road."

Now that I'm less shocked, I take in a beaten-up dusty trailer hitched to a General Motors Company truck in my driveway.

It can't have been a comfortable trip.

If they haven't heard from Sonia, why are they here? Really?

"I can't let you see Sara yet," I hedge. "You need to isolate in the trailer for ten days, first."

I can't see their mouths under the masks, but their eyes look deflated.

"We're willing to isolate," Olivia says. "Or we could go to the hospital and try to get tested, so we don't have to wait ten days."

I'm one hundred percent fine about being a hardass to these people. They should have emailed or at least snail mailed to let me know they were coming.

Forget the mail. What's so hard about picking up a phone?

Only the fact that we haven't spoken, in phone or in person, for months.

But I know if Sonia was here, she wouldn't want me to welcome them back into our lives.

Terence crosses his arms and looks at me. "You're a doctor. Is there any way you can use your influence to get us tested?"

"I can try," I say. "But for now, you'll have to wait in the trailer. It may take a while."

They nod, and this softens me.

"I'll make some calls," I say. Even though this is not my usual behavior. Especially during a pandemic. I feel a little bit sick that they're asking me to bend the rules for them.

They never should have come.

I wait until I see them disappear into their trailer, then I close and lock the front door. Now I am back inside our safe house.

Even though there was absolutely no touching, and we stayed six feet apart, I wash my hands and bathe them in hand sanitizer. Just to be sure.

Alessia is in the kitchen with Sara. I think they're making some kind of Italian cookie dough.

I explain what has happened. Alessia nods. She says something to Sara in Italian, which I think has the word grandparents in it. I recognize nonne and nonni, but my Italian verbs still need a lot of work.

Despite my better judgment, I phone the hospital and get tests set up for Sonia's parents through my lab buddies.

I call Terence and Olivia on their cell phone, even though I could go outside and knock on the door of their trailer. I give them directions to the hospital. I mention that I am calling in a favor to get this done for them.

"Is there a bakery nearby where we can stop and get cookies to thank your friends?" Olivia asks.

As far as I know, all the unique little restaurants and bakeries and stores in our neighborhood are closed, courtesy of the pandemic. I suggest they stop off at the neighborhood grocery and get some kind of generic gift basket.

"Will do," Olivia says. "Terence and I are heading out now."

I watch from the window and see their truck leave my driveway. The trailer stays.

I wonder if I have to offer them a guest room in the house or if they're planning on sleeping in the trailer.

Two more people for Alessia to feed and care for. Extra work for her. Emotional tumult for me.

How long is this visit going to last, anyway?

My friend Daniel expedites the tests and calls me when Olivia and Terence test negative. "They're on their way back to you," he says. "Just a heads up."

"I owe you one," I say. "I'm so sorry. Again, this was completely unexpected."

"Well, they seem like nice people, anyway," Daniel says. "Over achievers, maybe. They brought enough food to feed the entire department."

I look out the window and see Terence and Olivia pulling into our driveway again. This time, I get to the door before they ring the doorbell. Terence is carrying a bag of wrapped presents that must be for Sara.

"Please come in," I say formally. They're wearing masks, so I don't have to insist on that. I point to the gigantic bottle of 99.99% germ-killing sanitizer by the door and wordlessly they clean their hands.

Alessia appears in the hallway, holding Sara. She's changed Sara's clothes so now Sara is wearing her best ruffly pink dress instead of her usual shorts and top. She has a pink bow in her baby-fine hair.

Alessia hands Sara over to Olivia. Sara pulls Olivia's glasses off and puts them in her mouth. She looks proud of herself.

"Terence and Olivia, this is Alessia, Sara's nanny. Alessia, these nice people are Sara's grandparents," I say. "I guess Sara is making her own introductions."

But no one is paying attention to me anymore. They are all

absorbed in Sara worship. Clearly, Sara is enjoying all this attention.

I still don't understand why Sonia's parents are here. But maybe, this visit might be a better idea than I thought.

Chapter Seventeen

The past is a foreign country; they do things differently there. –LP Hartley, *The Go-Between*

Maybe I was right, and this visit is a really, really bad idea.

It's been two days now of pretending to welcome Olivia and Terence to our house. Two days of Olivia trying to get Alessia on her side. Two days of Terence talking to me about music.

I'm a doctor, not a musician. I guess it's his hobby or something. He brought Sara a bunch of tiny musical instruments. Maybe hoping I wouldn't notice them among all the other toys and clothes.

Or maybe Terence is trying to find out if I know enough to give Sara a good education in music, the way he educated Sonia's brother.

Either way, it's getting on my nerves. I haven't called Terence this—yet—but I think of him as an asshole.

We spend a lot of time in the back yard. Olivia loves pushing Sara on the baby swing. She holds her hands so Sara can baby walk around the climbing equipment. They bring out some of Sara's stuffies and have a baby tea party.

Terence takes a lot of pictures. He brings the musical instruments out, but all Sara does is put them in her mouth and drool on them. This pleases me.

I have to admit, Sara loves all the extra attention from her grandparents.

I'm glad somebody is happy.

The problem is, I still don't know why they're here.

After we put Sara to bed on the second night, I get tired of being patient.

Alessia has disappeared into the kitchen. She won't let Olivia help her cook or clean up. She makes it clear that Olivia and Terence are guests, who could never replace her.

All three of us are in the living room relaxing in front of the fireplace. Except I'm not relaxed at all.

Olivia can tell. She tries to placate me. "Terence and I are so grateful to you, Peter. For letting us spend this time with Sara," she says.

"She's a beautiful girl," Terence adds. "Just like her mother at that age."

That does it.

"You told me you haven't heard from Sonia since she left," I say slowly.

They're silent. What's wrong with them? Their daughter is missing. Why aren't they worried?

"I haven't heard from her either, but that's because she

told me not to contact her."

Olivia and Terence exchange glances. They're still wearing masks. Sara is the only one who doesn't wear a mask in our house. Maybe she's the only one with nothing to hide.

"What did she tell you?" I ask.

"Nothing, Peter. Sonia hasn't talked to us in person since your wedding," Olivia says. "When she left, she sent us a letter saying she is safe and asking us not to contact you."

Her hands twist in her lap. "We don't expect her to tell us anything. I think the only reason she talked at the wedding was to make you think we had a relatively normal relationship."

They're wrong about that. Sonia told me she wasn't close to her family before we got married.

I was fine with it. I figured I wouldn't see much of our in-laws. So what? But Sonia and I would start our own family.

We did start our own family. We still have a lot of work to do on it.

These two days with my in-laws are the longest amount of time I've ever spent with them. They're not evil. I guess. But...

"Why won't Sonia talk to you?" I ask.

Terence clears his throat. "Sonia is angry about something that happened before she left for nursing school."

"And what is that?" I ask. Full on doctor facade, hiding my nervousness and pretending to be an authority figure. Lucky I learned how to project that character in med school.

Olivia answers.

"Sonia told us that our neighbor across the street, a man

we've known for over twenty years now, came on to her. Very aggressively. She told him no, but she was frightened and shaken up."

"We didn't believe her," Terence adds.

"Why the hell not?"

I say hell instead of fuck in deference to their age. Because I think they're insane.

Why would Sonia make up a story like that? I'm confused by their reaction.

"This man and his wife used to have Sonia and Benedict over to their house to play in their pool with their own sons. All the kids grew up together."

Benedict is Sara's brother. He came to the wedding but left right after the ceremony. He said he had a gig.

Olivia and Terence were friends with this man. So they believed him over their own daughter?

I try to understand.

Not believing your own daughter is bad, of course, but is it worth breaking off a relationship with your family? And what does it have to do with Sara's brother?

She never calls him Benedict. Just "my brother." She rarely talks about him at all.

Is Sara over reacting? Whose side should I be on?

"Benedict didn't believe her, either," Terence says. "He accused Sonia of lying to get attention."

"Why would he think that?" I ask. "Sonia's not a liar."

Olivia and Terence look at each other.

"Benedict had just won an important award for one of his compositions," Terence said. "Also, he'd been accepted at

Juilliard. Looking back, we were pretty excited about it, and we weren't actually paying much attention to Sonia."

I try to look back at Sonia's childhood to imagine the way she must have felt. Hurt. Betrayed. Angry.

I understand now some of the jealousy she's expressed about her brother. I never took it seriously before. But what was it like growing up knowing her parents favored her brother?

"And that wasn't the end of it," Terence continues.

Wait. What?

A short pause. I assume they'll tell me the rest of the story, but they both look at the fire instead. No one says anything for a few minutes.

"So there's more?" I say finally. "What happened?"

Olivia makes eye contact with me, and this time, I can tell she is anguished despite her mask.

"A few weeks later, our neighbor was arrested for raping a girl Sonia knew at school."

"One of Sonia's friends," Terence adds. "She's never gotten over it."

I'm confused by the lack of antecedents. Who's never gotten over it? Sonia, or the friend?

"The friend committed suicide a month later," Olivia finishes.

Oh. Holy shit.

At least now I understand.

I should be on Sonia's side.

"I'm so sorry," I say. I have no idea what else to say.

"There was an autopsy," Terence says.

Oh, no. I don't want to hear this. I'm a doctor, I know what's coming.

"Her friend was pregnant," Terence finishes.

Jesus.

"You should have believed your daughter," I say very quietly.

Olivia nods. She's crying.

Too late now, Olivia.

"We were wrong about everything."

"Yes, you were," I say. I'm furious at them now. They hurt Sonia. Therefore, I want to murder them.

I start thinking about ways to make that happen. Painful ways that a physician would know, but a police officer would never guess.

Or maybe I should skip trying to be invisible and subtle. I can progress straight to the mythical comic book characters of my childhood. I want to swell up and throw Terence and Olivia out the window. I want my anger to turn me into The Hulk. I want to avenge Sonia the Marvel way.

Because what kind of parent behaves like this to their child?

"If we believed Sonia and took action in time, maybe the rape never would have happened."

Well—maybe.

We can't know that without a time machine.

I stand up. "I'm going for a drive. I need some air."

I can tell that Olivia and Terence know how angry I am, but they don't try to stop me from leaving.

I grab my keys from the hooks by the door and exit into

our well-appointed garage. Here are all my power tools. But no guns. That's fortunate right now.

I take the Lexus and drive to a park that's been empty since the pandemic started. I stare at the empty playground, wondering if I should go back home and order Sonia's parents to leave and never come back.

But then I'd hurt Sara. She benefits most from this relationship.

But I can't be polite to Terence and Olivia anymore. I want them gone.

I want to concentrate on Sonia.

On bringing her back.

I drive around the neighborhood for two hours before I am calm enough to go back to our house.

Olivia and Terence are still sitting in the living room. Waiting for my judgment.

"Knowing what you know now, if you could go back, what would you do?" I ask.

Not that I'm trying to excuse their behavior.

Terence looks at me. "Confront our neighbor? Punch him in the face? Tell him if he ever tries to get near our daughter again, we'll report him to the police?"

This is more than Terence has said to me during the entire visit.

All these reactions sound reasonable to me. If I could go back, I'd be even more violent. I'd punch the neighbor in the gonads.

Or maybe snip them right off.

"I don't know if you could have changed history," I say.

"The rape might have happened anyway. But your reaction would have made a difference to Sonia."

"Because she would know we believed her," Olivia summarizes.

There's nothing more to say. Except, where do we go from here?

Or do we go anywhere at all?

Is this the point where I rise like an outraged Victorian and bid them leave my house, never to return?

I can tell that Olivia and Terence are suffering. I have no idea how her brother feels.

There's no rule book that tells me how long a family should be punished for something terrible that they've done. It's not child abuse, but it's close. Because of the way they made Sonia feel.

I can feel my anger rising, maybe unfairly, at them.

Sonia's not here, and that's partially their fault. The way her family reacted years ago molds the way Sonia reacts to me now.

I do know that I have a part in what happened to our marriage. But it's easier to be angry at Terence and Olivia. At least I can do something about that.

"Did you ever apologize to Sonia?" I ask, my voice tight.

"Of course we did," Olivia says. "Many times."

"She hasn't forgiven us," Terence says unnecessarily.

I feel he's missing the point. The worst part is that Sonia hasn't forgiven herself.

That has to be why she never told me this secret. Something happened to her that changed everything.

I think Sonia was afraid I would stop loving her. Stop trusting her with Sara.

She left before this could happen.

Chapter Eighteen

"It would probably be good for you to get out of here,
but I asked more for my sake than for yours."
–Laurie Colwin, *Shine On, Bright & Dangerous Object*

At breakfast the next day, I ask Olivia and Terence to leave after they finish their coffee, fruit, and yogurt. I'm not a monster. I don't want them to starve.

On the other hand, I don't have any reason to be nice to them. I'm just not comfortable having them in my house anymore. Or in my driveway.

They don't offer much resistance. Their eyes look miserable above their masks. But they expect this.

"I need to sort this out," I tell them, and they don't pretend not to understand.

They give Sara big lingering hugs and kisses, which make her giggle. She doesn't understand why they look so sad. "I hope we'll see you again," Olivia says to me, and I take pleasure in not reacting at all to her words. Leaving the subject open.

I don't want to make promises I have no intention of keeping.

But most of all, I'm impatient for them to be gone so I can try to contact Sonia.

We stand outside. Alessia holds Sara and shows her how to wave goodbye. I don't wave at all.

I see Olivia look longingly out the window as Terence drives away.

And now they're gone.

Alessia takes Sara to the kitchen. I go back to my office so I can pretend to get some work done, but I can't concentrate.

Instead, I use the computer to find practicing private investigators and try to find the ones rated highest on Yelp.

There is no such listing on Yelp.

The internet advises people to find a private investigator that a friend or relative has worked with before. Obviously, they didn't think about what the fuck anyone is supposed to do if there is a pandemic.

I can't think of any friends or relatives who contacted a private investigator for any reason. However, when I put out a memo to my work colleagues, I receive four different recommendations.

I don't waste time wondering why other physicians at my hospital have taken advantages of these kind of services. Although since I have little work to do today, it's tempting.

I make a note to myself that no one's life is perfect, even when it looks that way from the outside. The way it does for my ridiculously rich and privileged colleagues.

Instead, I contact the only woman private investigator

recommended to me. For some reason, I feel less guilty about having a woman look for Sonia. Is it because I think women are less aggressive and intrusive than men? Or more likely to care about doing a good job?

I've waited too long to find Sonia. I pick up the phone and schedule a Zoom consultation with Patricia Morez, private investigator.

She turns out to be a pleasant, professional-looking woman wearing a purple jacket and flowery shirt. I change into a long-sleeved white shirt for this interview. I'm afraid she won't believe I'm a physician if she sees me in sweats.

I write out bullet points to keep myself on track. If I start to cry, I consult my bullet points. This works well.

Ms. Morez has a lot of questions. I don't have a lot of answers, but I give her as much information as possible.

Even when the questions are painful or embarrassing. As in, no, we weren't fighting before Sonia left. Yes, she seemed her normal self.

I give her Sonia's cell phone number, although I don't think it's been used since she left. She must have turned it off and bought a new one. The way a fugitive would.

Ms. Morez asks for social media data, but there are none. Sonia never posts to Facebook or Twitter or anything else. She hates all that stuff. Ms. Morez sounds skeptical when I explain this, but it's true.

Ms. Morez asks about bank accounts. I give her our joint bank information, but there haven't been any withdrawals since Sonia left. I suggest that she has found a job and is supporting herself from the money she makes as a nurse.

Ms. Morez wants to know if Sonia took the car with her, so she can trace it, but I explain that Sonia left the car in the garage. I think she walked downtown, took a taxi, and paid in cash.

Then Ms. Morez asks for all Sonia's professional information. I don't know this stuff by heart, but I do the best I can.

I know Sonia keeps her nursing license with her high school and college diploma in a silver tin on the floor of our bedroom closet. But when I take these papers out, I realize Sonia took the license with her. Which makes sense if she planned in advance to get a job.

Ms. Morez says not to worry, she can get Sonia's nursing license by contacting the nursing board. It will just take a little longer.

I take pictures of the pages of the long note that Sonia left for me and send them to Ms. Morez. I email the most recent pictures of Sonia I have. They're from a barbecue we went to a week or so before she left.

Sonia is wearing a white sundress and red sandals. She looks beautiful.

Every time I look at a picture of Sonia, I have an increased sense of loss. And now I wonder why I was such a forbearing idiot in the first place. Why did I wait this long to find her?

I need her to come home.

But Ms. Morez makes it clear that her job is to find Sonia, not to bring her home. If and when she finds her, that will be my responsibility.

I ask for an estimate on how long it will take her to find

Sonia, and what my chances are. I already have a good idea of how much it will cost.

"I'll start working on this right away," Ms. Morez says. "You'll receive a written report of my progress every week."

I have to be content with that. But I've never been the most patient man in the world. This first week of waiting is very long.

I try to make the time go faster by concentrating on work, such as it is.

I scour Amazon to try to find new baby toys for Sara. I sit on the carpet with her building block castles.

Sara demolishes them in a single move, sometimes before I finish building them. We both think this is very funny. Alessia seems less amused because she's the one who gathers up the far-flung blocks from all the corners of the room.

I feel guilty, so I take the unprecedented step of buying Alessia a new set of gardening tools. She's startled, but she thanks me.

I get Sara a gardening hat, some tiny shovels and trowels, and a wheelbarrow so we can help in the garden.

Sara likes getting wheeled around outside. I don't know how much help we actually provide. But it makes me feel better to spend time with my daughter outside. Away from the television and her gigantic toybox.

If we plant something, I think Alessia digs it up and replants it when we're not looking.

I admit we might be putting the seeds in upside down.

The first week goes by, then the second.

There's no news.

Every week, I wait for the progress reports, but they're more like bills detailing step by step what's been done. I can see that Ms. Morez is good at her job, but mostly her reports say where she hasn't found Sonia: at the morgue, for example. I suppose I should be grateful for that.

I get a postcard from Olivia and Terence telling me they reached home safely. I throw it away, but then I rescue it from the wastebasket and stick it into my bureau.

I'm not sure why. Maybe to show Sonia if she ever comes home. Or maybe to have a backup plan if Sonia never does make it home.

If Ms. Morez can't find her, what are my options? Do I keep Olivia and Terence at a distance to honor Sonia's memory?

Or do I let Sara get to know her grandparents because that will make her childhood more normal?

I don't know what to do. And I'm very far from feeling I can trust Olivia and Terence with Sara.

I would trust my own parents, but they are sensibly staying home and trying to get through the pandemic. They are petrified of getting sick. And I don't blame them.

Alessia and I display Sara to my parents during FaceTime meetings every week. She smiles and waves and babbles in front of them, but she has no idea who they are.

This physical separation is the worst part of the pandemic for me. Well, death would be worse, but I haven't experienced that yet, personally. Except when I examine x-rays for the virus. I'm getting a lot of those.

After I make my reports, I don't like to think what happens to the people who belong to the radiology.

Anyway, because of Ms. Morez's efforts, I'm pretty sure Sonia is alive. Somewhere. So far. She's made it through this part of the pandemic.

I feel as grateful as I feel angry about that.

Chapter Nineteen

"I ought to have thought of the people who had no armour." –T.H. White, *The Once and Future King*

I don't have a lot of friends. Just a few guys that I grew up with—and a small number I met in medical school—and a minority of colleagues who became friends at work.

Less than ten people altogether, probably. I've never counted.

Partly because we're guys and we don't get into mushy stuff. We act so differently from women. We don't keep track of all our life events so we can celebrate them.

We're not insensitive, though. If someone gets divorced, usually we find out about it and we try to give each other support. For me, that means saying, either in person or via email, if you feel like talking, you know you can tell me anything.

But usually, we don't feel like talking. If someone does,

that means they feel like crying, and unless it's a funeral, I'm not really into that stuff.

If it's a funeral, it depends on whose funeral.

I mean, there have been way too many funerals this year already. I feel as if 2020 is the year of the funeral.

So, when my friend Colin calls me from work, I figure it's something I don't want to know about. Something with emotions involved.

Colin leaves me a message to call him back. I pretend to forget.

Then, while Alessia and I are in the backyard with Sara, he calls again. Of course, it's while I'm changing Sara's diaper.

It's a messy moment so I don't have time to look at my phone. I answer it automatically and press the audio button without looking.

"Peter. You trying to avoid me?"

"Yes, I am, Colin. I talk to you practically every day on Zoom. Can't this wait until our next meeting?"

(This is how guys who are friends talk to each other. Or, at least, how radiologists do it).

Sara lets out a scream, but it's not because she is stung by a bee or anything. She just likes to scream sometimes. She thinks it's funny.

"Is that Sara? How's she doing?"

"Sara's doing great," I report. "Growing smellier by the minute until I finish changing her diaper. So, what do you need, Colin?"

"Well, I know we haven't seen each other since the pandemic started, but you remember my dog, Chloe?"

I'm a little confused because usually Colin and I don't talk about anything except difficult patients. These days, we have a lot of them.

I vaguely remember having drinks with Colin in his backyard months ago. He has a dog who might be a collie. She likes me to throw a Frisbee for her.

"Is Chloe okay?" I ask. I trust Colin's not going to tell me Chloe is sick or has died.

"She's fine, except about two months ago, she had five puppies unexpectedly. We're trying to find homes for them, hopefully homes with children. I know you and Sonia don't have any pets, so I thought you might—"

Oh, no.

"Maybe when Sara gets older," I hedge. "Right now, I think a puppy would be hard to manage with such a young baby."

"Everyone says that, but you know Milos in cardiology? He has one-year-old twins, not that much older than Sara, and they took two puppies last week. Young dogs are great with children."

"I don't know, Colin. I'll talk to Sonia about it but I'm pretty sure she feels Sara ought to be at least four years old before we get a dog."

I hope to God Alessia doesn't understand what I am saying.

I am going to hell.

I am a liar.

I never told Colin or anyone else at work about Sonia leaving.

It doesn't seem necessary because first, I think she will come back, and second, how will anyone know she's gone since we can't leave our homes?

I'm sure Colin can tell from my tone of voice that Sonia and I have never discussed getting a dog. She likes cats, and I am okay with them, but I wouldn't want cat hair all over the house. And Sara is too young to know not to pull a cat's tail. She might get scratched, at her age.

"Oh." Colin is uncharacteristically quiet. But not for long.

"Maybe you can put Sonia on the phone?" he suggests. "I'd love to tell her about these puppies. I think I can get her to change her mind."

"She's not going to change her mind, Colin," I say regretfully. "Neither am I."

"But the pandemic is the perfect time to adopt a pet," Colin argues. "Everyone says so. We're all home now and we have more time to train an animal."

This is all my fault. God is punishing me for being a liar.

"Sonia's busy right now," I say. "But I'll come over and look at the puppies, Colin. I'm not making any promises, though."

"You won't be sorry. What's a good time for you, Peter?"

We arrange for me to check out the puppies at four o'clock this afternoon. Colin says he'll put them in the back yard so I can see them in action.

I tell myself I'll go over and tell Colin how cute the puppies are, then go home.

I don't take my mask off when I get out of the car. If I smile at the puppies, I don't want Colin to see.

Colin has a big fenced-in back yard, and right now, there are three puppies running around in it. They're a lot bigger and more active than I expected.

I look at Chloe, who's sitting on the deck watching them. She's what I would call a medium size dog. From the looks of these puppies, they're going to outgrow her in weeks.

"Hey, Peter. Glad you could make it." Colin is watering his garden. He waves me into the yard. "I thought you'd bring Sonia and Sara so you could all see the puppies."

"They don't know much about dogs, but they trust me to pick out a good one," I lie.

Except I have no intention of doing that.

"They're all good. Are you more interested in a boy or a girl?"

"A boy." Because vaguely I know girl puppies go into heat and that's how Chloe landed in this mess.

"Do you know who the father is?" I ask Colin.

"God knows. There are so many dogs on this block. I have no idea how the damn dog got inside our garden."

Kind of like the rabbits and our backyard.

I figure if the dog was able to leap over Peter's well-kept fence, it must be a huge dog. I don't know that many dog breeds, but maybe a Newfoundland? Or some kind of giant shepherd, the shaggy kind?

I'm pretty sure Alessia will not welcome a large mutt with a loud bark. And all three of these puppies are barking loudly as they compete for a squeaky toy.

Yet somehow, a half hour later, I'm leaving with one of the puppies. He's brown and fluffy and has big sad brown puppy eyes.

I'm hooked.

Colin generously throws in a collar and leash and a gigantic bag of dog kibble. It will take a few days until any puppy supplies I order online arrive at our house.

Most importantly, I ask Colin for a copy of last week's *New York Times*. Colin watches me spread thick layers of newspaper all over my car before I let the puppy go inside.

Colin shakes his head, but doesn't say anything, just waves goodbye.

I believe I can order car seat and floor protectors designed especially for puppies, but until they arrive, there's no way I'm letting this puppy anywhere near my leather seats.

Unfortunately, the puppy takes the newspaper as a challenge, and by the time we've made the short drive to my house, he's chewed, vomited, urinated, and defecated on every major article this week.

Not that the news was worth saving.

I just pray the layers were thick enough that nothing got through.

I find the perfect name for the puppy, though: Oskar, as in Felix and Oscar, the odd couple. I spell it with a k, not a c, in case the puppy decides to be his own dog and turns out to be unusually neat.

That would be nice, wouldn't it?

I decide to act as if bringing home a puppy is nothing out of the ordinary. As if I have a hope in hell of pulling this off.

When I get home, Alessia and Sara are in the kitchen making dinner.

As soon as Sara sees the puppy, she babbles with joy and holds her arms out so she can babyhandle him.

"Stai scherzando," Alessia says, the expression on her face considerably less welcoming than the one on Sara's face.

"Isn't he great?" I say desperately. "Il sumo nome e` Oskar."

Alessia looks at the puppy licking Sara's face as hard as she is licking him in return. The effect is joyous but unsanitary.

"I know what you're thinking, Alessia, but don't worry. I'll take care of Oskar," I assure her. "I don't want to make any extra work for you."

"Portare fuori il cane," Alessia says as Oskar pees on her clean kitchen floor.

"No, no, Oskar." I pull him outside and try to get him to pee in the backyard, but now he's more interested in racing around as far as the leash allows him to go.

I can tell Oskar will be a great addition to our family, but it may take a while for him to really understand his new role.

The atmosphere at dinner is tenser than usual. Oskar is shut in the den with a bowl of water which he promptly knocks over.

Hoping Alessia won't notice, I mop up the water and refill the bowl. I remind myself to order dog supplies tonight, including a bowl that can't be knocked over.

If there is such a thing.

I give him Oskar an old slipper to chew on until I can get some real toys.

Nevertheless, Oskar whimpers pathetically through dinner, which does not bode well for any of us sleeping tonight.

After dinner, we all go outside and have a moderately successful play session.

That is, Sara tries to pet Oskar, and he tries to wash her face and hands and feet.

The result is a cascade of giggles and happy barking.

Alessia does not look impressed.

After all, she has to calm Sara down at night, give her a bath, and help her get to sleep. I show up after Sara is in bed to sing and tell stories only if there is a problem.

Well, tonight, there is a problem.

Sara refuses to go to sleep, even to lie down, until Oskar is curled up on the rug in her room.

I can tell Alessia does not approve of this arrangement, but I assure her that I will order a dog bed and hopefully it will arrive tomorrow.

I'm not sure Alessia understands what I'm saying, as she still looks dour. But I sing Sara her favorite songs, then go to my office, and hope for a peaceful night.

I spend several hundred dollars online ordering every possible piece of equipment to make life with a puppy less stressful before I finally go to bed.

I check on Oskar and Sara. She has stuck her hand out through her crib and is holding onto Oskar's fur, but he seems fine with it.

And the night is peaceful, until two in the morning, when Oskar vomits up a lot of grass and some of Sara's rug, which he has destroyed in the night.

Amazingly, Sara doesn't wake up.

And amazingly, Oskar doesn't bark. I clean up the vomit

and make a soft nest for him with some bath towels.

I will get in trouble for this tomorrow with Alessia.

Oskar wags his tail so hard I'm afraid the tail will fall off, but then he lies down against Sara's crib.

I pat his head. When I look up, Alessia is in the doorway.

"Due angeli dormienti," she says softly.

"Si," I agree. They do look angelic. For now.

Chapter Twenty

There walked in beauty on the island a maiden named
Andrea. –James Thurber, *The Wonderful O*

I am patient for several months after Sonia leaves home.
Until one day my patience is gone. Maybe forever.

Now I wake up angry and go to sleep angry.

Everyone thinks of me as a calm, reasonable guy. A doctor.
Someone who never expresses much emotion.

They don't know me at all.

I want to go back in time and murder the man who did this
to Sonia. Murder him in the most painful way possible.

If that's really why she left. Because how do I know?

There must be more to this story, but I'm too angry to
figure it out.

Maybe it's because Sonia hasn't contacted me in such a
long time.

It makes me feel she's never coming back.

I try to hide how I feel from my family and colleagues.

Most importantly, I try not to take these feelings out on Sara and Alessia.

I keep myself extra busy with my job, so I don't have time to think—well, obsess—about Sonia.

That doesn't work.

After months of dreaming about Sonia and waking up to find the bed empty next to me, I start thinking about dating.

Someone. Else.

Dating's probably not the right word. Getting to know someone.

Because let's be honest, isn't that what Sonia is doing?

In all probability?

Every time I think about seeing someone else, though, I get worried.

How can I be sure of being safe?

Am I inviting infection?

Can I minimize risk without offending the other person?

Dating was bad enough before the pandemic. Now, if I go on a date, I might risk dying. Because how do I know I can trust the other person?

I thought I could trust Sonia. If I was wrong about her, will I be wrong about everyone else I meet?

But I'm a physician. And still young. Ish.

I should be able to find someone who lets me set the rules.

If we both agree on wearing masks and having a negative test and dating exclusivity, it might be all right.

Or maybe just stick to video dating at first.

Until we feel comfortable with each other.

If that time ever comes.

I tell myself that the hardest part is beginning. But I keep putting it off.

When I'm at the hospital, though, I do ask the nurses about their favorite dating apps.

"I'm stunned, Doctor," one of the nosier nurses says. She pokes me in the chest. "Is there something you want to tell us? Aren't you married? Didn't your wife have a baby just a few months ago?"

"Oh, it's not for me," I say lamely. "I'm doing research for Sara so I can keep her safe. I heard girls start having boyfriends at age two now."

I'm not sure the nurses believe me, but they give me inside information about the apps.

There's one nurse who's particularly helpful. She sits next to me and scrolls through the apps patiently, explaining the pros and cons of each one.

She's very pretty. Red hair and aqua-blue eyes. Although I've heard that some women wear colored contact lenses now, so I'm not sure if her eyes are brown in real life.

She'd still be pretty. With brown eyes. She'd look a little bit more like Oskar.

I don't dare even think about glancing at her breasts. Thank God the air conditioning is on and she's wearing a cardigan.

Her name is Ingrid. And she smells good. Like French toast. Emphasis on the French.

I wonder if I should ask Ingrid to have coffee with me.

But what if it turns out we don't like each other? We'll still have to work together.

No. I'll stick to the apps.

Although whoever designed these apps wanted to torture men. There are way too many apps, and they are far too confusing.

I don't like the idea of having something like this on my phone, where it can be discovered.

Also, I don't want to be interrupted during the day with potential matches. If this means I miss some interesting people because I don't want to devote all my time to this nonsense, so be it.

I decide not to put a picture of myself on the app, and I use an assumed name.

God forbid anyone from the hospital sees me and asks for a date.

I create a fictious profile, too. I say I'm a physician, of course, because I think that might be an attractive trait. But I don't mention my family at all. And I don't put in any information that might make someone who knows me suspicious.

I take my time getting started. I tell myself that, at the very least, looking into dating will distract me from thinking about Sonia.

And, if it doesn't work out, no one has to know.

Finally, at night, after Sara goes to bed, I look through the apps in my office, on my computer.

I pick one app and decide to stick to it.

I find a few women who might be compatible. But how do I know they really care about the same values I care about?

And how do I know they're telling the truth about what they like doing on a date?

I guess at some point I have to trust that people are who they say they are.

But I'm not telling the truth, so why should they?

The difference is, I would never hurt anyone. If someone turns out to be perfect for me, I will reveal my identity.

Although, if a woman finds out that I am still married and my wife is missing and I have a kid, she'll run for the hills.

Right? Because I'm not so attractive that Sonia wanted to stick with me.

I go through several nights of agonizing over whether I'm doing the right thing or making a mistake that I'll regret the rest of my life.

Finally, I convince myself there's no harm in starting out slowly. And cautiously.

I send a conservative message to three different women, hoping one of them might be interested. I think courtly might be one way to describe my approach.

I ask them to meet with me over Zoom for fifteen minutes. I call it a first impressions date.

Who knew? I get three messages back, all positive, within an hour.

I'm so surprised, I stand up at my desk and accidentally pull the cord out of my power source, knocking the computer onto the ground.

Unfortunately, I also knock my gigantic glass of water all over it and break the glass.

Swearing, I go to find the upstairs vacuum and a towel so I can clean up the damage.

In the hallway, I look over the banister. I see Alessia

downstairs with Oskar.

She's detaching his leash from his collar. Did she take him for a walk?

Does Alessia secretly like Oskar?

But before I can decide, I realize that Alessia is smoking a cigarette.

Oh. My. God.

Alessia can see me in the hallway upstairs, but she turns her head, ignoring me. She sits down on the couch, inhales, and blows smoke into Oskar's face.

He must be addicted to nicotine too because he's trying unsuccessfully to jump into Alessia's lap and wash her nose off.

I wonder if Oskar is depressed because so far, he hasn't been successful at anything.

Well, he did get me to bring him home.

Ordinarily, I would march downstairs and give Alessia a strong lecture on the dangers of smoking. I do not want her smoking near Sara!

But I've never seen her smoke before, or even smelled smoke on her, and I wonder if she's smoking because Oskar is such a stressful companion.

Anyway, first I need to dry off my computer and vacuum up the broken glass before someone gets hurt.

The lecture will have to wait.

And then I set up times to meet with each of these three women. Even though the thought of it terrifies me.

I write out a script of questions that I can use if inspiration dries up. Also, a couple of sentences that focus on whether the woman and I want to proceed to another meeting.

I'll put the script in my lap so I can see it, but no one else can.

I don't want to hurt anyone's feelings by starting something and then ending it after one Zoom. But I want to be professional and tactful if it doesn't work out.

I change my shirt three times before the first meeting. I also put on jeans instead of sweatpants because I don't know what angle her camera is set at, and I don't want to seem underdressed.

Then I realize if the woman can see my jeans, she can see my script. I tape it to the side of my computer instead, well off camera.

I also try to position my own camera so it will be looking into her eyes, not even remotely close to her breasts. But that's a fruitless exercise. I wish I had an IT guy here.

The first woman is not my type. She's blond and as thin as a model, and she has two little vertical lines between her eyes that never relax.

I don't feel comfortable talking with her, but I manage to get through the scheduled fifteen minutes. We talk about our jobs, (she is a pharmaceutical sales representative) and where we live, (she lives in Madison, New Jersey) and how hard it is to date during the pandemic.

At the end she asks if I want to set up another meeting, and I say, "I'm very new at this. Let me think about it and get back to you either way," as I don't want to leave her without any hope at all.

My plan is to send her a polite email saying I have decided

to move in a different direction and thanking her for her time.

But she must be familiar with this strategy from other dates. She hangs up frowning, the two little lines deep and angry and accusing between her eyes.

I realize that men can be as disappointing as women.

And maybe, in some situations, like online dating, men have more power.

The world isn't fair.

The second meeting goes more smoothly. This woman is older, and more interesting. She's not wearing any makeup that I can see, and her nails are unmanicured, unlike the first woman.

She's an archaeologist whose divorce became final just before the pandemic. Her name is Helen, and we joke about the obvious classical inference.

"Thank God my parents didn't name me Pythia. Obviously, I'm no oracle," she says wryly. "I wanted to be alone, but not pandemic degree of alone."

We have a relaxed conversation, and I almost enjoy talking to her. This one seems busy and confident and happy except for being lonely.

The only problem is that she's not Sonia.

So, I repeat my prepared wrap up from the first interview because I'm just not sure about moving ahead.

However, this conversation ends on a friendlier note than the first one. I feel we might progress further.

If I can wave a magic wand and turn her into Sonia, we will.

The third meeting starts out better than the first, but not

as well as the second.

I wonder if this is because I feel the slightest bit of attraction to Helen after the second meeting, so I'm less open to possibilities in this meeting.

The third woman is a registered dietitian who lives in Maine. She has two dogs, and I can hear one of them barking in the background. A deep unhappy bark, as if he's telling her to stay the hell away from me.

And maybe he's right, because this is a perfectly nice woman, but she has no appeal for me.

Fortunately, I don't think she minds at all when I wrap things up a bit early, not waiting the full fifteen minutes. I send her my rote email and get a polite thanks anyway in return. There's just no chemistry.

There is with Helen.

But I'm just not sure what to do next.

The good news is, I have a little reprieve, because Helen is teaching a class at Columbia (remotely of course) but she told me she would be too busy to have another meeting for the next two weeks.

I'm relieved that I don't have to contact Helen right away. And, as much as I hate to admit it, that may be a sign I shouldn't pursue her.

But I don't send her my carefully crafted get-out-of-jail-free email right away. I want to leave things open in case I change my mind.

Or in case Sonia comes back. Because let's face it, that's what I really want.

Isn't it?

Chapter Twenty-One

I had that sensation which sometimes comes to us all, of
returning to a situation that had already been resolved on
some previous occasion, of being again committed to a
tragic course of action, having learned nothing from that
other time or those other times.
–Paul Scott, *The Jewel in the Crown*

I have never been good at waiting.

Is anyone?

At the end of July, I think that Sonia will be found in
August.

Sara and Alyssa and I spend August playing in the backyard. I buy a baby pool for her to splash in when it's too hot
and humid to use the swing.

I order sandbox toys: pails and shovels and strainers made
of bright-colored plastic. Alyssa and I teach Sara to build a
sandcastle using wet sand.

I learn Italian phrases to use when Sara throws sand:

"Macché! Ma anche no!" By the end of summer, she starts to understand us, or at least our disapproving expressions.

During the last weeks of August, I think that Sonia will be found in September.

In early September, Sara starts pulling herself up using the bars of her crib. When I come into her room to change her in the morning, she's clutching the bars, soaking wet, unsteady but proud.

Sara starts leaving bite marks on the bars of the crib. I double-check on the internet to make sure this brand of crib is covered with lead-free paint, and it is. Whew.

Sara's top incisors peek through her gums when she smiles. Alessia gives her the hard end of a loaf of Italian bread to chew on.

I worry that Sara will choke, and convey this to Alessia, but she looks at me with such scorn I stop talking. And Sara is fine.

I spend a lot of time raking the yard because it's boring but gives me something to do outside.

I should be using this time to become less impatient, more the kind of man that Sonia wants to return to. But instead, I am grouchy and withdrawn.

Adversity does not make me admirable.

Toward the middle of October, I look at baby costumes online. There will be no trick or treating this year because of the pandemic. But I can dress Sara up and take pictures of her first Halloween.

I try to describe the American observance of Halloween to Alessia. I explain that it won't occur until the last day of

October, but I show her the bumblebee costume I'm thinking of buying for Sara.

By now, Alessia is used to me planning everything early. She probably thinks I'm crazy, but I haven't learned the Italian for most of her muttered phrases yet.

"Dolcetto o scherzetto?" Alessia says unexpectedly. She shrugs.

She doesn't look enthused about the costume. I wonder if she's ever sewn a costume for her own children or grandchildren. I can't ask her to sew one for Sara, though. That's too much.

Sewing costumes is the sort of thing I thought Sonia would do with Sara this year. Along with making her own baby food after Sara stopped wanting to nurse.

Sonia missed all this earth mother stuff. I wonder if wearing a commercial costume and eating Italian food at such a young age will be stuff Sara remembers and resents when she gets older.

Stuff to tell her therapist.

When I think about it, carving a pumpkin and dressing Sara up just so we can commemorate her first Halloween all by herself is probably a stupid idea.

Then again, this whole year has been stupid.

But before I order the costume (in two sizes, because I'm not sure how it will fit since Sara is tall for her age) I get an email from Ms. Morez.

It's not my usual progress or, as I call them, lack of progress report.

She asks me to set up a Zoom meeting.

I try to Zoom her right back, but no, she's not available.

I have to pick from several hours listed as open on her website, and the first one is at eleven a.m., our time, tomorrow.

Waiting for this appointment is almost unbearable. It's raining. I can't even take Sara outside.

Waiting isn't so bad when Sonia is here. She's good at distracting me with long games of Scrabble and complicated plans to take Sara to museums and parks when she gets older.

I still have a notebook filled with lists of age-appropriate equipment and activities for Sara at every age up to sixteen. I believe that's when Sara turns into a pumpkin and hates us.

Unless Sonia never comes back and then, maybe, Sara will recognize what a selfless father I am and love me forever.

Or not.

I've checked off all the age-appropriate books and toys recommended by experts for Sara during babyhood. Alessia makes me order fabric bins so she can teach Sara to clean up after she plays.

Sara hates cleaning up. I did too, at her age. Well, I still do.

But I don't want Alessia to be angry at me, so Sara and I cover the floor of her room with plastic toys and then I show her how to throw the pieces back into the bins. She misses most of the time. I'm pretty sure she's missing on purpose.

I carry Sara to the window to watch the rain. I sing "Piove, piove," followed by "Rain, rain, go away," because after all, Sara has to learn English, too. Sonia will think it's strange if Sara only understands Italian when she sees her again.

There's no way to make the time go faster. It passes in its

own way, on its own terms. Time goes particularly slowly when I lie awake at night willing the alarm to go off.

I am twenty minutes early for my Zoom meeting the next day. I test all the computer equipment as it is sure to malfunction since this is an important meeting.

It must be. Ms. Morez has never done this before.

I am right.

Ms. Morez starts the meeting by telling me she has found Sonia. She doesn't smile, but I do. A big goofy smile that feels unfamiliar on my face.

This is the way my world changes, with a simple address to write down.

Then I stop smiling because I think I'm having a panic attack. I'm having trouble breathing. My heart is beating so fast I feel like a hummingbird.

Deep breaths, as I would tell my patients. Some of them react this way when I read their x-rays and find cancer.

Others cry. Or faint.

I tell myself I am stronger than that.

Ms. Morez explains the steps she took to get Sonia's current address, but I barely listen. I'm focused on getting out of the house and bringing Sonia home.

I can be ready to leave by about three p.m. this afternoon.

Of course, there are a few logistics that need to be resolved first.

I thank Ms. Morez fervently when I can breathe and talk again.

She says she hopes everything works out for us.

It must.

If I fail to bring Sonia home, our marriage is over.

I've stopped trusting her to come home by herself. Even if the pandemic is the reason she hasn't returned already. As opposed to me. Or Sara.

I end the Zoom meeting and open a Word document on my computer. I need to create a list so I can make this trip successful.

Masks. Hand sanitizer. Travelling toothbrush (I have a case that holds the brush and paste). Clothes. Food that won't spoil in the car.

Extra pillows and blankets.

I don't worry about shaving because like every other man on earth, I have grown a beard during the pandemic. Sara likes to pull at it, so I might keep it.

Unless Sonia hates it. Or maybe because she will.

I want her to be surprised when she sees me.

To see how I've changed.

I will take the Lexus even though it gets terrible gas mileage because it is comfortable for long trips. I can stop at rest stops to use the facilities and sleep in the back seat instead of taking the risk of getting sick at a hotel.

I plan the route using Google maps. It's about a two-day drive from here. I could get there in a few hours flying, but I'm not brave enough to get on a plane in the middle of a pandemic. Even though some airlines are operating again, and a lot of foolish people are flying.

Not my parents. Nobody I know.

It's too dangerous to fly.

I want this trip to be so safe, it's boring. Because maybe I'll be able to breathe then.

I expect to stop every two hours. I'll get out of the car and walk around for at least five minutes. It won't help if I have an accident because I'm tired and driving carelessly.

Sonia didn't head for New York or Boston. She's in Pennsylvania, in a small town close to Bryn Mawr. I have her address. I can bring her home in our car.

Sonia hates this car. She thinks it's a status symbol and is embarrassed to drive it. But even Sonia admits the Lexus is much more comfortable than her Subaru.

Which she left in the garage, and it's still sitting there.

Well, I drive it at least once a week. Just short distances to keep the tires from losing pressure and the battery from dying.

I drive it to the park. I sit in the lot watching ghosts by the swings.

The Subaru smells like Sonia if you sit in the front seat. But I can't think about that now.

I clear my calendar for a couple of days at work. I'll take my computer, phone, and some extra power cords in case somehow, I lose one, or a cord stops working. If a patient has an emergency, I can work on the road.

It doesn't take me long to pack.

But I spend an hour trying to figure out what to say to Alessia.

I don't want to lie to her.

But I'm afraid if I tell her I'm bringing Sonia home, she'll leave and go back to Italy.

I want Alessia to stay. To make life easier for Sonia. And

to make life easier for Sara. Because it will take a while for the mother and the daughter to get used to each other again.

Won't it?

I honestly don't know.

I do know that now, Sara notices when I leave the house. Even if Alessia holds her, she wants to come with me if I go in the backyard.

I think Sara will notice that I am going away for a few days.

Maybe that's why I should get Sonia back as quickly as possible. Before Sara starts to think that Alessia is her mother. She's outgrowing the baby phase where anyone can take care of her.

I tell Alessia the truth.

I explain that I will be back in a few days, and I expect Sara's mother to be with me. I ask Alessia to commit to staying with us for at least another six months.

And probably longer. A lot longer.

Alessia doesn't say no.

There's already a sheet taped to the refrigerator with all the emergency numbers including my cell phone. Not that we've called anyone during the pandemic.

I check that the pantry and freezer and refrigerator are full from the last Instacart delivery. I make sure that Alessia knows how to call me on the cell phone I gave her. I showed her this months ago, but now would be a very bad time to forget.

I stress the importance of always keeping the cell phone in the pocket of her apron in case I need to reach her. Or in case she needs to reach me.

Alessia stands there listening and holding Sara on her hip. Then she passes Sara to me so I can say goodbye.

This is the worst part.

Naturally, Sara decides to have a full-blown meltdown, throwing herself around in my arms and screaming bloody murder.

Children are never cute and loving when you need them to be.

I remind myself that I'm doing this for Sara as well as for myself. For Sonia. For our family.

Alessia takes Sara back and nods for me to go.

I can hear Sara screaming as I back out of the garage.

If Sonia stayed, this wouldn't be happening.

I'm off to make sure it never happens again.

If I can believe that.

Chapter Twenty-Two

For Jack's part, getting married had settled something in
him, seemingly paving the long stretch of highway ahead
upon which we could cruise for the rest of our lives.
–Adrienne Brodeur, *Wild Game*

Day One

I'm on the road. Not knowing what comes next, but in
pursuit.

This first day of driving will be a short one. I plan to
stop when it gets dark tonight. I hate driving in the dark almost as much as I hate driving with the sun in my eyes.

Fortunately, I keep two pairs of sunglasses in the glove
compartment. It's perhaps the only part of the Lexus that is
upholstered in vinyl instead of leather. On the inside only, of
course. The outside is the same semi-aniline leather as the rest
of the dashboard.

I put one of my pairs of sunglasses on the empty seat next
to me in case I need them. But right now, the weather is

cloudy in that menacing just because you're driving, don't think I won't thunderstorm if I feel like it way.

Sonia holds my sunglasses for me when we drive together. I imagine making this same trip back to the house, this time, with Sonia next to me.

It's only a few days away.

I don't feel like listening to music. I'm being careful with the Global Positioning System screen because driving to Pennsylvania is unfamiliar for me. It's not a state I ever dreamed about visiting.

I have no idea why Sonia chose Pennsylvania to run to. Unless she thought I would never think of following her here.

Finding myself in Pennsylvania is as likely as me finding myself taking sky-diving lessons.

But for a town in Pennsylvania, Bryn Mawr is not all that bad. A nice college. Several hospitals in the Bryn Mawr area. Public transportation to Philadelphia. I looked it up on Google before starting the drive.

Bryn Mawr is a Welsh name that means "big hill." Maybe that's why Sonia picked it. She has a thing about Wales and Scotland and Ireland.

I even found a Google Earth picture of the apartment building where Sonia is living. There's plenty of parking. The apartment building looks a little run down, and it's too close to the railroad station for my taste. I don't like train or traffic noise when I am trying to concentrate. But I will say, her apartment is in a nice neighborhood with lots of trees and a park nearby.

It wouldn't be like Sonia to pick a luxury apartment. This

place looks more like her than our home does. Way more granola.

Is it frustrating for Sonia that I have much more upscale taste than she does? Is that part of what made her feel so uncomfortable, she left me?

For a moment I wonder if she will want to leave this new apartment community. But my job is to remind her of Sara and make her want to go.

In case reminding her of me and our life together isn't enough.

I'm not hungry, but I plan to take scheduled breaks to stay alert while I'm driving. In the evening, I get off the highway and find a rest stop that's almost totally empty. I doubt police officers will bother me about parking too long during the pandemic. I'm not taking someone else's spot.

I find a picnic table and have water and two granola bars for dinner. The bars are a little stale—I took them out of our pantry, and they've been sitting there since before the pandemic started—and so crumbly I'm thankful to be eating outside, not making a mess in my car.

When I get apprehensive, when I have a job to do, I lose my appetite. This is all I need to keep me going until breakfast tomorrow. I eat the bars while I watch the sun set.

I haven't seen a sunset in a long time, despite being home for so many days during the pandemic. As darkness comes, I wonder why I haven't made room for something so beautiful in my life.

My excuse is that if I'm outside, I have to be alert to every move Sara makes. But I could watch the sunrise, maybe, while she is still sleeping.

There are always a lot of shooting stars during the month of August. It's almost October now, so I missed that opportunity this year. But I could take Sara outside to look at the stars when she wakes up at night. Instead of listening for Alessia to go to her to calm her down.

I should make a point of doing these things when Sonia and I drive back. It's not too late. Is it?

I wear gloves and a mask when I go into the men's room. Whoever takes care of this place keeps it very clean, and I'm grateful. I leave a twenty-dollar tip to express my appreciation. It's a bit over the top, but maybe being generous will bring me good luck with Sonia.

Now dark shadows are replacing red streaks in the sunset. There's no way I'm driving anymore tonight.

I curl up on the wide soft leather backseat of the Lexus, making sure all the doors are locked. I have my phone and pillows and blankets.

It's not like being at home, but it's a little more comfortable than going camping. Maybe.

I call Alessia to make sure she's paying attention to my instructions about keeping the cell phone close in case of emergency. She answers after one ring.

"Alessia, it's Peter," I say. Come on. Who else would it be?

"Sara asleep," Alessia says. "Una bambina stanca."

A tired baby. I wish I was there to kiss her goodnight.

"Everything's all right?" I ask. Alessia grunts in response.

Well, I didn't hire her for her conversational skills. Which, I remind myself, are better than mine in Italian.

"I'll call earlier tomorrow," I say. "So I can talk to Sara."

Day Two

I wake up when the sky lightens. This is early for me. At home, I have blackout shades so I can sleep longer. I'm a little disoriented but eager to get back on the road.

I take some time to watch the sunrise and when it becomes clear that today, I'll need those sunglasses waiting for me in the front seat, I get up.

My legs and back are stiff from sleeping in an unaccustomed curled up position, but it's a small sacrifice to make in exchange for bringing Sonia home.

I put on a fresh mask. There are only two other cars in the parking lot, but I don't want to run into someone who's sick and doesn't know it yet.

I see a man walking his dog in the distance. It makes me wonder how Oskar is doing. I hope Alessia is good to him, and he doesn't miss me too much. It might be fun to bring Oskar on a long road trip when he gets older and is better behaved. Right now, I don't trust him not to ruin the inside of my car.

I use the restroom and change my clothes in the not-so-roomy booth. I don't want people to think I'm weird, changing my clothes in the car. Although my windows are darkened, so they probably can't see inside. But just in case.

The vending machines in the lobby don't offer a lot of choices for breakfast. I pick a blueberry muffin probably full of sugar and the wrong kind of fat and warm it up in the microwave. I get two cups of (terrible) coffee and wash down the muffin at the picnic table.

At least I get to start the day outside, seeing grass and trees and insects up close. I admire the job someone's done on the rest stop lawn. Now it's time to get back to distance driving.

Today, the route seems less complicated. I take a risk and turn on the radio. The news is full of promises about a vaccine, but no firm dates as to when it will become available. I brace myself because the way things are going, it could take another year.

It's a long day. Squinting into the sun. Following the Global Positioning System so I don't get mesmerized by the highway and make a wrong turn. Stopping every two hours to take a break.

There's very little traffic on the road. Once, a herd of deer crosses the road in front of me, but far enough away so I don't hit them. They look like ballet dancers leaping across the highway. It's the prettiest thing I see all day.

I remember there are bears in Pennsylvania. I hope I don't run into one who wants to sample the food in my car.

By lunchtime, I'm bored.

I find another rest stop that's bigger and fancier and more crowded than the first one. It has a fast-food court, so I treat myself to a chicken sandwich. Protein. Sort of. I'm feeling sorry for myself, so I get an order of onion rings, too.

I go outside with my food, grabbing lots of napkins. The food court is full of happy or happyish families, and it makes me sad to eat by myself. Also, I want to take my mask off so I can hear and speak clearly when I call Alessia.

This time, the phone rings several times before she

answers it, growling "Ciao." I can hear Oskar barking and Sara having a tantrum in the background. Has she stopped crying since I left? Except for when she fell asleep?

"Hello, Alessia, it's Peter. What's going on with Sara?"

"You talk," Alessia says in the least accented English I've heard from her. Now Sara is howling into my ear.

"Wait a minute, Alessia, let me talk to Oskar first." I hear Alessia snort, but she puts the phone next to Oskar, so the crying is muffled, and the barking is much louder. I order Oskar to go to his bed. Somewhat to my surprise, that works and the barking stops.

"Alessia, please put Sara back on," I ask. My daughter is still sobbing.

"Sara, this is Daddy. Why are you crying, young lady?"

Of course, she can't tell me, and this is not as easy to fix as talking to Oskar.

I sing her a song that she likes, "All the Pretty Little Horses," but it doesn't help much.

Alessia comes back on the line. "Sara has fever," she says. "Coughing and crying. Getting worse. You coming home now?"

I'm horrified because there's nothing I can do at this distance.

"I'll be home soon," I promise. "Call me if Sara gets worse, Alessia."

But she hangs up without saying goodbye.

I get back in the car, somehow feeling as if I'm getting whatever Sara has. Or maybe just food poisoning. And that makes me feel pissed.

It's somehow Sonia's fault that I had a lousy lunch. I notice my eyeballs feel grainy as if someone wrote on them.

Now I have to drive until I get to Sonia's apartment. I have to be careful not to have an accident because I'm worried about Sara. That's Sonia's fault, too.

I drive for a while, then I stop to call Alessia again. My mood doesn't improve when I hear that Sara still has a fever, and her cough is getting worse. I don't hear crying this time, but I have a sense of foreboding.

"I'll be home as soon as possible," I tell Alessia. "The first part of the trip is almost over."

I can feel her skepticism through the phone.

"You come home for Sara now," she orders. "No more waiting."

I stop taking breaks and just drive. This makes no sense as Sonia may be working during the day. If I get to her place and she's not home, I'll be stuck waiting in my car unless I can persuade a superintendent to let me into her apartment.

And I don't think I feel comfortable doing that.

I'm coming prepared, though.

I've brought gifts from home: a tin of cookies baked by Alessia. A digital photo frame full of pictures of Sara.

There's no way Sonia will be able to resist me and my presents.

Probably.

When I get to Bryn Mawr, I look around the small-town streets. There's not a lot of people walking around and even fewer going inside shops. Everyone wears a mask, so it's hard to see if they're smiling or downcast.

It takes me a while to find a florist. A surprised attendant makes me a gigantic mixed bouquet of wildflowers (I think?) at Be At Your Best Flowers.

They're expensive but it's the middle of the pandemic and I'm thankful this store is open. If I didn't buy these flowers, I expect they would be sent to one of the hospitals or more likely, to a funeral.

Sonia is not the type of woman who likes diamond jewelry or cashmere sweaters. Or, needless to say, fur coats. I'd buy those, too if I thought it would get me anywhere. I just know they won't.

While I'm downtown, I fill up with gas because of the long drive home.

I arrive at Sonia's apartment a bit earlier than I expect to. It's about two fifteen in the afternoon because I haven't stopped driving since my early and unsatisfactory lunch.

I'm not hungry. My hands are icy cold.

I put the photo frame and cookies in my backpack, and I carry the flowers to Sonia's apartment door. I check that I have the right address because I don't want to bother a stranger.

I knock at the address Ms. Morez gave me, and at first, I think there's no one home. I may have wasted all that money on the flowers for nothing.

Anticlimax, my middle name.

Then Sonia opens the door.

Chapter Twenty-Three

She wasn't doing a thing that I could see, except standing there leaning on the balcony rail holding the universe together. –J.D. Salinger, *A Girl I Knew*

Then Sonia opens the door. She's wearing blue jeans and a dark green cotton sweater. Her feet are bare. Her hair is braided into one thick plait and still reaches all the way down to her waist.

I could look at her forever.

It's not just the way she looks. It's the way she is. Without her, I feel like a robot. I'm animated only when she appears.

I can't be my precise orderly self unless I'm balanced by Sonia's singularity.

Her Sonianess stabilizes me.

I never want to be away from her again.

I know I should be furious at Sonia. But I'm so grateful to see her I get a huge lump in my throat.

"Peter?" she says uncertainly.

I hold out the flowers. She takes them from me automatically.

Bad move on my part. I can't kiss her or hug her with the flowers between us.

"It's good to see you, Sonia," I say. "May I come in?"

"Yes, come in," she says, opening the door further. "I don't mean to be rude, Peter. I'm a little surprised. I wasn't expecting you."

"I know."

I step into her living room. It's pretty much what I expect. Very small and cozy. Not much furniture. What there is looks secondhand.

But it's nice. Somehow disordered and neat at the same time.

Lots of books and fossils on display. A cat gets up from a butterfly chair and disappears into another room when it sees me.

A cat.

Great.

But of course, Sonia doesn't know about Oskar.

"I have a vase somewhere in the kitchen," she says. "I'll be right back. Let me put these into some water. They're beautiful."

I follow her into the kitchen. It's only a few steps from the living room.

The kitchen is also very small and a bit shabby.

"Your apartment is very nice," I say. "Have you lived here since you left?"

"Yes."

"It looks like you enjoyed fixing it up."

Sonia isn't paying attention to me. She's looking for a vase under the sink.

Finally, she finds one for the flowers and sets the arrangement in the middle of the kitchen table.

There doesn't seem to be a dining room. And the flowers are definitely the prettiest thing in the kitchen.

Not that I'm judging. But I wonder if I should offer to take her out to lunch. To a nice restaurant where we'll be on neutral ground.

"I was afraid you might be working," I say. "Is now a good time to talk?"

"I don't have to be at work until five this afternoon," Sonia says. "So we can talk for a little while."

Sonia leads me back into the living room. We sit down next to each other on the obviously Ikea sofa. It's not very comfortable but I'm more concerned that I still haven't kissed her.

"You look great," I say. I want to say she looks beautiful, but I don't know if I'm still allowed to comment on her appearance. "How have you been?"

Sonia looks down at her lap. "I've been fine, Peter," she says. "How about you? And Sara?"

I clear my throat. I reach for her hand. I haven't held Sonia's hand in such a long time. She doesn't immediately take it away. Maybe that's a good sign.

"We haven't been fine," I say, "without you."

She looks at me, but I don't give her a chance to talk.

"We've missed you," I say. "More than I've ever missed anyone. Did you miss us, Sonia?"

"Of course I did," Sonia says.

"Then why did you leave, Sonia?"

She has no ready answer.

"I mean, did you miss me," I clarify. "As much as Sara. Because she's your daughter, so I'm pretty sure you missed her, but I'm your husband."

Good job, Peter, getting that legal clarification straight. Are you trying to make your wife walk out the door again?

"I did miss you," Sara says softly.

I clear my throat again. "Were you trying to get away from me? Did I do something wrong to make you leave?"

"No, Peter," Sonia says. She takes my other hand, the first time she has touched me voluntarily since she left. "It wasn't because of you or Sara."

"Then was it because of your neighbor? And what he did to you and your friend?"

Sonia snatches away both hands and stands up, glaring at me.

"How did you find out about that?"

"Your parents visited," I said. "They told me what happened. And it's not your fault, Sonia."

"They came to our house?"

"In the middle of a pandemic," I confirm.

"How dare they!"

"Yes, that's what I thought too," I agree. "I knew you wouldn't want them there. I sent them away."

"Thank you," Sonia says, and for the first time she sounds like the real Sonia, not a robot who's practiced saying the right things.

"Can we talk about this?" I ask. "Because this is why you left, isn't it?"

Sonia nods.

"You blame yourself for your friend's suicide," I continue. "But like I said, it wasn't your fault. And blaming yourself just hurts me and Sara."

Sonia sits down again. "I never meant to do that," she says. "I thought I was helping both of you by going away. Because I couldn't be a good mother."

Now Sonia looks dazed. I reach out and take her hand again.

"Sara and I thought you were a great mother," I say.

"I'm just trying to get used to you knowing about this," she says. "It's been a secret for so long."

"Why didn't you tell me?" I ask.

Sonia looks incredulous. "If I told you, you wouldn't love me anymore."

"But I know now. And I still love you," I argue. "You can trust me, Sonia."

But I can tell she doesn't. At least, not yet.

But she's sitting in the same room with me. Not running away. We're holding hands.

"Can we talk about it?" I ask again. "Can you tell me how it happened?"

Sonia looks at the floor.

"I was wearing a blue dress that was a little bit too tight," she says. "I thought it was the perfect color for me. Mr. Zachon said I looked beautiful in it, and that made me feel good. Because my brother and my parents never noticed things like that."

She looks at me.

"Everyone was talking and laughing and eating dinner. They were talking about my brother getting into Juilliard. But Mr. Zachon wasn't. He was the only one paying attention to me."

She swallows.

"He kept stroking my leg under the table. Getting higher and higher, until he was touching inside my panties."

I rub her back gently.

"I moved my leg away as far as I could, but I was too embarrassed to say anything.

"And then, after dinner, he grabbed my arm in the hallway while my parents and his wife and my brother were still having drinks in the living room. He squeezed my breasts. It hurt. He told me he was the only one who saw how beautiful I was."

"What a fucking bastard," I say quietly.

"I said, 'No, your wife is in the living room, Mr. Zachon.' But he grabbed me and tried to kiss me. I pulled back and wiped my mouth off. And after he and his wife left, I told my parents about it. But they didn't believe me."

"I believe you," I say. "They should have believed you."

Sonia looks at me. "But I couldn't stop it, Peter," she says, her voice shaking. "I wasn't strong enough to stop it. And if I wasn't strong enough then, how can I be a good mother now?"

"You're a different person now," I say. "Before, you didn't have anyone on your side. But now you have me. And Sara.

We make you stronger."

Sonia shakes her head. "Not strong enough to go back and change the past."

She's crying now, and I put her head on my shoulder and hold her. She cries for a long time.

My other hand searches for a handkerchief in my pocket. Sonia's face is red and shiny. Tears and snot from her nose are getting on my good shirt.

This is real grief, not movie grief. There's nothing pretty about it. Even a mask can't hide it or make it look good.

"I don't care about the past, Sonia," I tell her. "I only care about what's happening now with you and me and Sara. Can we try to fix this so you can be with us again?"

Sonia blows her nose on my handkerchief. "I don't know," she says. "I don't know what to do."

"We need to get you help," I say. "Maybe that means talking to someone, a professional."

"No." Sonia looks at me defiantly. "That's not going to help me feel better. It won't make a difference to anyone except me."

And me and Sara, I think. But I don't argue.

"Then maybe you have to do something harder," I suggest. "Like going back to your friend's family and talking to them about it. Telling them how sorry you are you didn't report that bastard to the police."

Sonia looks aghast. "I can't do that," she says. Not "I'll try to do that," or "I'll think about doing that." Just a flat denial.

"Why not?" I'm trying to be patient and supportive.

It's getting harder because I feel as if she's using the past to ruin whatever present and future we might have.

"They hate me," Sonia says. "Jackie was my friend, and I betrayed her. Worse than that. It's my fault she's dead."

"No, Sonia. It's not your fault. You were a victim, too."

Sonia turns away. "That's not an excuse."

"All right. But it's still not your fault. What could you have done that would have changed anything?"

I look her in the eye.

"No one would have listened to you because you were just a kid. It was your parents' responsibility to stop it, not yours," I say. "They didn't tell your friends, or the police. And that's why the fucking bastard got away with it."

I can tell she's not listening to me. I'm down to my last resort.

"You left, Sonia, because you can't forgive yourself. But you're not the only one suffering. Sara and I are, too."

She looks at me with pain in her eyes but doesn't say anything.

"Would you at least come back with me for a few days?" I ask. "So we can talk?"

I can see this is a big ask.

"I wasn't expecting any of this today, Peter," she says. "Can you give me a few days to think about it? Maybe you can stay at a hotel downtown while I try to decide?"

No.

No trying to decide.

"I can't stay that long, Sonia." I see the tension in her shoulders. "But what if I find something to do by myself for a little while? A bookstore or a coffee shop or something. And then I'll come back, and you can tell me your decision."

I don't like this idea, and I can tell Sonia doesn't like it either. But she nods.

I don't want to be away from her for even one minute. But I can see she has a lot to turn over and agonize and think about.

"While you're gone, I'll call work and tell them I need some time off for a family emergency," Sonia says.

"Okay. I'll be back in a couple of hours."

I fish the cookies and the photo frame out of my backpack and leave them on her coffee table.

I hope I'm doing the right thing.

I hope I can trust Sonia not to pack up and disappear while I'm downtown.

I give her the longest two hours in the history of time.

There's a nice secondhand bookstore in Bryn Mawr. It's as good a place as any to wait while your wife decides the future of your family.

This is something I wanted us to do together.

But I can't change Sonia from someone who lives inside her head.

This is a big part of who she is. This is one of the reasons why I love her.

Most of the time.

Right now, I feel more exasperation than love.

I can't concentrate on any of the books I find. When I take a break for coffee, I can't taste it.

I call Alessia to check on Sara, and now I start to panic, because Alessia says Sara is coughing and not eating or drinking. Her fever is still rising.

I can't stand being away a minute longer, so I go back to the apartment.

For once, I didn't make a mistake. Sonia is still there when I get back.

But just as I thought, the first thing she says is, "I need more time, Peter."

Enough.

"I can't wait any longer, Sonia," I say as gently as possible. "I have to get back now because Sara is sick. Come back with me and we'll talk after we're sure Sara is getting better."

Sonia whirls around. "Sara has coronavirus? Is that why you're here?"

"No, it's not COVID. I would never leave if Sara had the virus."

I can tell Sonia's listening to me now. Finally.

"Sara's running a fever," I explain. "She's getting worse. It might be some sort of infection. I don't know because she got sick after I left."

I don't want to lie and make it sound as if Sara is sicker than she really is, because that might be the only way to make Sonia come home. But if I lie, I'm just asking her to walk out the door again. Then again, this is the worst possible time to be away from my daughter, when she's not feeling well.

"Did you leave Sara with Jan and Ted?" Sonia asked. "And now she's sick?"

"She's not with Jan and Ted. I had to get help after you left," I defend myself. "But even the best help isn't the same as being with your parents."

Sonia glares at me. "You should have told me the minute you arrived. We're wasting time. We should be on the road already."

She looks around the room wildly. "I have to get ready. Can you get Chaos into her travel crate?"

"Uh…Chaos?"

"The cat," Sonia snaps. "Can you help, please?"

"Uh…sure?"

A cat named Chaos. This is not a good sign.

I open my mouth to tell Sonia about Oskar, but then I shut it again.

Oskar can wait until we get home. In fact, the entire universe can wait.

I'm not sure if Sara is coming home because she thinks Sara is sick or if Sara being sick is the excuse she is making because she already wants to come home with me.

Then again, what does it matter? Sonia is coming home with me.

Sonia rushes into her bedroom to pack some clothes. I follow her to ask if she got some emergency family time off while I was at the bookstore. She snaps, "Yes!"

Sonia doesn't sound too happy. Maybe she isn't as sure about coming home as I want her to be.

I don't know exactly how we got to this point. But I want to keep going, and I don't want to stop until we're home.

Somehow, I get the white cat into the travel crate. Essentially, I throw a towel over her and stuff her in.

It turns out that Chaos is a perfect name for this cat. I have to pull her out from under the bed and I get scratched pretty badly in the process.

But so what? Sonia is coming home with me.

I did it.

I can't believe it.

I'm afraid to say anything in case Sonia changes her mind.

But she doesn't.

In less than ten minutes, we lock the door of the apartment and buckle the seat belt around Chaos in the back seat. The cat is yowling. Will she make that noise all the way home?

I know better than to say anything.

Sonia puts a suitcase in the trunk. It has some sort of vacuum tube sticking out the side. I look at her, perplexed.

"For the cat hair," she says.

Oh.

Sonia slides into the front seat next to me. She holds my sunglasses in case I need them. "Go," she says urgently.

I set the GPS and turn the key in the ignition.

Sara is sick.

Sonia hasn't forgiven herself.

Alessia is going to kill me when I walk in with a cat.

I haven't even mentioned Alessia to Sonia.

I remind myself of all these negatives because I don't think I've ever felt happier in my life.

Part Three: Sonia and Peter
(and Sara and Alessia and
Oskar and Chaos)

Chapter Twenty-Four

Innocent, the mere wishing of a mere wish.
–Jeannette Haien, *The All of It*

I want to visit Bali during monsoon season. No, I'm not crazy! I think hotels are cheaper during this time, and the rain will lead to cooler temperatures. I don't mind wandering around in a raincoat and rubber boots. After all, I'm not exactly a beach person.

Usually when I travel, I want to visit a place where I can find birds and animals I've never seen before. But Bali is different.

My destination is Ubud, a place famous for art. Not war, sex, rock n' roll or drugs. The sculptors who live here are famous. I love that idea!

I plan to meet artisans who sculpt animals and mythological creatures. I already have a winged cat made from Albesia wood. I'll be on the lookout for another flying animal to come home with me. Or a shadow puppet. Oh, it's so hard to decide, and I'm not even there yet.

Of course, I'm not flying thousands of miles just for the shopping. While I'm in Ubud, I'll scout out the Monkey Forest. There are over one hundred different kinds of trees in it! Since I like to photograph trees, I may have to spend an entire day there.

Also, the forest is a sanctuary for long-tailed macaque monkeys. I'd love to see them leaping from tree to tree. The next best thing to flying. They can be aggressive, so it's important to remember not to bring any food with you that might set them off. I won't make that mistake.

I'm thinking of making a reservation at Artotel Haniman Ubud. They have an airport shuttle so even if I'm totally jetlagged when I arrive, I can sit back and relax until we reach the hotel. Also, I'm told there's a fancy coffeemaker in every room. Just the thought makes me feel I'm on vacation.

I'm walking from room to room doing some light dusting, thinking about Bali and not paying much attention to time. I know I have a couple of hours before I have to leave for work. So, when someone knocks at the door, my first thought is that it's a kid selling candy bars to raise money for school. Of course, I'll buy at least one bar. Maybe several so I can give them away at work and be a hero.

I look for my purse, and of course, I can't find it. I'm a little late getting to the door, but the kid is polite, not hammering and yelling the way some of them do.

Because I'm not paying attention, I miss that sign.

Then I open the door.

To the last person in the world I expect to see.

"Peter?" I say uncertainly.

He holds out a gigantic arrangement of wildflowers. I take them from him automatically.

It's like having a forest between us. He leans over as if he wants a kiss or a hug, but he can't reach me.

Maybe that's a good thing. Is he angry? He seems very calm and collected for someone who just travelled such a long way.

For nothing?

"It's good to see you, Sonia," he says. "May I come in?"

"Yes, come in," I say, opening the door further. "I don't mean to be rude, Peter. I'm a little surprised. I wasn't expecting you."

That's an understatement.

"I know."

I feel an overwhelming urge to kiss and hug him, but I can't tell if this is real or just the tail end of emotion from seeing someone I married and lived with. Someone I knew very well, and yes, have missed.

I don't move closer to him, though, because I don't want to give him unrealistic expectations.

He steps into the living room. He doesn't look as uncomfortable and from another world as I thought he would here.

Then again, Peter is uncharacteristically a bit travelworn. Maybe that helps him fit in.

My cat is not a fan of unfamiliar humans, and when she looks at Peter, she judges him to be a stranger. Maybe a bad guy. Chaos gets up from the butterfly chair and disappears into another room.

Peter doesn't exactly look thrilled either when he notices

Chaos. Well, that's too damn bad.

When Peter and I were first married, I asked if we could get a cat. But first he said he didn't want the mess of cat hair on the sofa, and then, when Sara came, he was afraid an animal might scratch or bite her.

Maybe I could have presented my arguments for a pet instead of running away and adopting a cat. Too late now.

Anyway, I don't think Peter should feel afraid of Chaos. She's a gentle, shy cat, the opposite of her name. I named her Chaos for fun. To make people apprehensive in case I ever have guests.

And there are special vacuums designed to get rid of cat hair. I have one and the sofa looks fine.

"I have a vase somewhere in the kitchen," I say. "I'll be right back. Let me put these into some water. They're beautiful."

Instead of listening to me (I said I'll be right back) Peter follows me into the kitchen.

I guess he hasn't learned to listen yet. The kitchen is very small, and I don't feel comfortable with the two of us in it. I feel crowded and Peter hasn't even been here for five minutes.

"Your apartment is very nice," he says. "Have you lived here since you left?"

"Yes."

"It looks like you enjoyed fixing it up."

I'm not paying attention to him. I'm looking for a vase under the sink. If he feels neglected, that's his problem. I asked him to wait for me in the living room, after all.

Finally, I find a vase big enough for the flowers and set the arrangement in the middle of the kitchen table.

They look a little out of place. Maybe because the arrangement is so big and elaborate, it dwarfs everything else in the kitchen and makes my table and folding wooden chairs look cheap.

"I was afraid you might be working," Peter says. "Is now a good time to talk?"

"I don't have to be at work until five this afternoon," I say. "So we can talk for a little while."

Actually, I don't have to be at work until seven p.m. today, but I don't want to get into a long, emotional conversation with Peter. I have my own plans for the day.

I lead Peter back into the living room. We sit down next to each other on the sofa. I hope he's comfortable.

Then again, if he's not comfortable, he can leave. Since I didn't invite him here.

"You look great," Peter says. "How have you been?"

I look down at my lap. "I've been fine, Peter," I say. "How about you? And Sara?"

Peter clears his throat. He reaches for my hand.

I haven't held Peter's hand in such a long time. I don't immediately take it away. Maybe I should, though. I'm not positive we're still on hand-holding terms.

"We haven't been fine," he says, "without you."

I look at him, but he doesn't give me a chance to talk.

"We've missed you," Peter says. "More than I've ever missed anyone. Did you miss us, Sonia?"

"Of course I did," I say without checking to see if it's true.

But I think it is.

"Then why did you leave, Sonia?"

I have no ready answer. It's complicated.

"I mean, did you miss me," Peter clarifies. "As much as Sara. Because she's your daughter, so I'm pretty sure you missed her, but I'm your husband."

"I did miss you," I say softly. Because I realize it's true. I feel better with Peter in the room.

As if something I lost and have been looking for a long time finally showed up. Something I wanted and needed.

He clears his throat again. "Were you trying to get away from me? Did I do something wrong to make you leave?"

"No, Peter," I say. I take his other hand, the first time I have voluntarily touched him since I left. "It wasn't because of you or Sara."

"Then was it because of your neighbor? And what he did to you and your friend?"

Wait, what?

I snatch my hands away from him and stand up, glaring.

"How did you find out about that?"

"Your parents visited," he says. "They told me what happened. And it's not your fault, Sonia."

"They came to our house?"

"In the middle of a pandemic," Peter confirms.

"How dare they!" I'm so angry I'm having trouble breathing.

"Yes, that's what I thought too," Peter agrees. "I knew you wouldn't want them there. I sent them away."

"Thank you," I say. And I really mean it. For once, he did

the right thing without me telling him what to do.

"Can we talk about this?" Peter asks. "Because this is why you left, isn't it?"

I don't want to talk about it. But I nod. Because he sent my parents away.

"You blame yourself for your friend's suicide," Peter continues. "But like I said, it wasn't your fault. And blaming yourself just hurts me and Sara."

I sit down again. Because I did not expect him to say that.

I'm not sure if it's true, but if it is, I'm an even worse person than I think I am.

"I never meant to hurt you," I say. "I thought I was helping both of you by going away. Because I couldn't be a good mother, I couldn't be a good person around Sara."

Now Peter reaches out and takes my hand again. We're touching again and I can't lie and say I don't feel anything.

"Sara and I thought you were a great mother," Peter says.

"I'm just trying to get used to you knowing about this," I say. "It's been a secret for so long."

"Why didn't you tell me?" Peter asks.

He can't be serious.

"If I told you, you wouldn't love me anymore."

"But I know now. And I still love you," he argues. "You can trust me, Sonia."

There are a lot of feelings in this room right now. Trust isn't one of them.

But Peter is sitting in the same room with me. He's not running away. We're holding hands.

"Can we talk about it?" he asks again. "Can you tell me

how it happened?"

I look at the floor. It will be easier if I don't see his face when I tell him. Let's get this over with.

I might as well tell him and then he can leave.

I'll never see him again once he knows.

"I was wearing a blue dress that was a little bit too tight," I say. "I thought it was the perfect color for me. Mr. Zachon said I looked beautiful in it, and that made me feel good. Because my brother and my parents never noticed things like that."

I look at Peter to make sure he's listening. So he doesn't miss the bad part.

"Everyone was talking and laughing and eating dinner. They were talking about my brother getting into Juilliard. But Mr. Zachon wasn't. He was the only one paying attention to me."

Just saying the words makes me want to vomit. I swallow to keep my breakfast down.

"He kept stroking my leg under the table. Getting higher and higher, until he was touching inside my panties."

Peter rubs my back gently. He does that when I'm upset. It helps.

"I moved my leg away as far as I could, but I was too embarrassed to say anything.

"And then, after dinner, he grabbed my arm in the hallway while my parents and his wife and my brother were still having drinks in the living room. He squeezed my breasts. It hurt. He told me he was the only one who saw how beautiful I was."

"What a fucking bastard," Peter says.

"I said, 'No, your wife is downstairs, Mr. Zachon.' But he grabbed me and tried to kiss me. I pulled back and wiped my mouth off. And after he and his wife left, I told my parents about it. But they didn't believe me."

"I believe you," Peter says. "They should have believed you."

That's not the worst part. He needs to understand so he'll understand why I left.

"But I couldn't stop it, Peter," I say. "I wasn't strong enough to stop it. And if I wasn't strong enough then, how can I be a good mother now?"

I've been very clear. Now he knows. He should get up and leave now.

But he's still here. Why?

"You're a different person now," Peter says. "Before, you didn't have anyone on your side. But now you have me. And Sara. We make you stronger."

I shake my head. "Not strong enough to go back and change the past."

I've avoided this for so long because thinking about it makes me relive it.

I start to cry. Peter puts my head on his shoulder and holds me.

I cry for a long time until his shirt is wet and gross. He hates for anything to mess up his good shirts. That hasn't changed.

But it feels good to be held.

Peter gives me a handkerchief.

"I don't care about the past, Sonia," he tells me. "I only care about what's happening now with you and me and Sara. Can we try to fix this so you can be with us again?"

I blow my nose and ruin his handkerchief. But he doesn't look mad.

"I don't know," I say. "I don't know what to do."

"We need to get you help," Peter says. "Maybe that means talking to someone, a professional."

"No." It was bad enough talking to Peter. I'm not going through this again with a stranger.

"That's not going to help me feel better," I say. "It won't make a difference to anyone except me."

Peter doesn't argue.

"Then maybe you have to do something harder," he suggests. "Like going back to your friend's family and talking to them about it. Telling them how sorry you are you didn't report that bastard to the police."

"I can't do that."

"Why not?" I can tell Peter is trying to be patient and supportive. But he wasn't there when it happened. He doesn't know what it was like.

"They hate me," I explain. "Jackie was my friend, and I betrayed her. Worse than that. It's my fault she's dead."

"No, Sonia. It's not your fault. You were a victim, too."

Yes, but I'm still alive. I turn away. "That's not an excuse."

"All right. But it's still not your fault." Peter says. What could you have done that would have changed anything?"

Of course it's my fault!

He makes me look at him, even though I don't want to. I

just want him to leave.

"No one would have listened to you because you were just a kid. It was your parents' responsibility to stop it, not yours," Peter says. "They didn't tell your friends, or the police. And that's why the fucking bastard got away with it.

"You left, Sonia, because you can't forgive yourself. But you're not the only one suffering. Sara and I are, too."

He said that before, and it makes everything even worse.

"Would you at least come back with me for a few days?" Peter asks. "So we can talk?"

There's no way I'm going back with him.

But I don't want to hurt his feelings. He came all this way and he's been nice to me. Even though he should hate me now.

I don't understand his behavior.

"I wasn't expecting any of this today, Peter," I say. "Can you give me a few days to think about it? Maybe you can find a hotel downtown while I try to decide?"

"I can't stay that long, Sonia."

Well, go then.

"But what if I find something to do by myself for a little while? A bookstore or a coffee shop or something. And then I'll come back, and you can tell me your decision."

I don't like this idea, and I can tell Peter doesn't like it either.

But I nod. Because I need time to myself.

And I don't want him to know I've already decided not to go back with him.

"While you're gone, I'll call work and tell them I need some time off for a family emergency," I tell him.

I can do that. I have so much time off. I can take a few days because I never do.

I won't go back with him. I'll stay here. But calling in to work will make Peter think that I'm being reasonable.

"Okay. I'll be back in a couple of hours."

He kisses me before he gets up from the sofa. He puts a tin of cookies on the coffee table.

I know he didn't bake the cookies. And I'm not hungry.

Peter also hands me an expensive digital photo frame. He's trying to impress me, and it's not going to work. I would have been just as happy looking at photos on his phone.

I will look at the pictures after he leaves, though. Because probably these are mostly pictures of Sara.

And then, finally, Peter walks out the door without asking for his handkerchief back.

I'll wash it while he's gone.

Although I wouldn't be surprised if I never see him again.

And I have to talk myself out of packing a suitcase and driving away again.

I don't because Peter was nice to me. But it's hard.

I put his handkerchief in the wash, and I call work to get some time off. It's easier than I think it will be.

If I spend all this time off in my apartment, by myself, I can travel and calm myself down. I can stop thinking about what Peter forced me to tell him.

I don't want to think about it anymore.

Part of me wants to spend the rest of the day travelling. All right. Escaping.

Instead, I take the time to look at photos of Sara.

She's gotten so big!

And she's doing so much more now. Smiling and playing with baby toys and even standing in some of the pictures.

Holding on to the rail of her crib but still standing.

There's an old lady in the background in some of the pictures. Is she the woman Peter hired to take care of Sara?

Was he careful? Did he check her background?

Maybe she's the one who baked the cookies.

I open the tin and sniff. The cookies are very elaborate. Someone spent a lot of time in the kitchen.

In my kitchen?

I nibble on a chocolate lacy cookie, and almost fall off the couch. They are so good!

I end up eating two. I can't help it.

I hope I'm doing the right thing. Not going back.

I scroll through all the pictures of Sara on the digital photo frame.

I wish I could put the pictures in chronological order. There must be some way to do that. I'll have to ask Peter when he comes back. Right now, the pictures are just scrolling through the frame randomly.

If I ask Peter to arrange the pictures one way, they will tell the story of Sara getting older.

But first, I want to be able to focus on the baby pictures. At about the time I left.

Does she miss me?

When I left, I thought Sara was so young, she wouldn't miss me.

But she's getting older now. Even if that old lady takes good care of her, she might start to miss me.

I didn't think I'd spend this day eating cookies and thinking about the future of our family.

I almost wish Peter was still here so we could do this together.

And then he knocks at the door.

He's only been gone a couple of hours.

I can't stall anymore.

He sees I've been looking at the pictures in the photo frame. I should have turned it off and put it away.

It's hard to look at him, so I look at the pictures.

"I need more time, Peter," I tell him.

"I can't wait any longer, Sonia," he says gently. "I have to get back now because Sara is sick. Come back with me and we'll talk after we're sure Sara is getting better."

What did you just say?

"Sara has coronavirus? Is that why you're here?"

"No, it's not coronavirus. I never would have left if Sara had the virus," Peter says, trying to reassure me.

I feel as if I'm having a heart attack. What is going on?

"Sara's running a fever," he explains. "It might be some sort of infection. I don't know because she got sick after I left."

Is Sara really sick? Or is Peter lying to get me to come home?

Would he do that?

"Did you leave Sara with Jan and Ted?" I ask. "And now she's sick?"

"She's not with Jan and Ted. I had to get help after you left," Peter defends himself. "But even the best help isn't the same as being with your parents."

I glare at him. "You should have told me the minute you got here. We're wasting time. We should be on the road now."

Why didn't he tell me this the second he walked in the door? Doesn't he know how important Sara is to me?

Well, maybe I haven't given him any reason to believe that.

And maybe I didn't believe it myself until just now.

Now I have to change all my plans.

I didn't expect to spend this day eating cookies, looking at pictures of Sara, and now packing. But I have no choice.

Is this what I really want to do? No, of course not.

This isn't about me changing my plans. It's about Sara.

"I have to get ready. Can you get Chaos into her travel crate?"

Peter looks confused. "Uh…Chaos?"

"The cat," I snap. "Can you help, please?"

"Uh…sure?"

I rush into my bedroom to pack some clothes. Once again, instead of taking care of Chaos the way I asked him to, Peter follows me.

I don't want him in my bedroom. I have to pack. Quickly.

Peter asks me if I already called work to get some time off, and I snap at him.

Maybe I'll apologize later. Maybe not.

I don't know exactly how we got to this point. But if Sara is sick, this changes everything.

What I want doesn't matter anymore.

And what I don't want is for Peter to stop driving until we're home.

Peter is not very good with animals. But Chaos is such a sweet cat and so easy to handle.

I hear some meowing, but when I come out with my suitcase, Chaos is in her travel crate.

This is my last chance to change my mind.

But I don't. I'm coming home with Peter.

I tell myself it's only for a few days. To make sure Sara is all right.

In less than ten minutes, we lock the door of the apartment and buckle the seat belt around Chaos in the back seat.

She's still meowing. She'll probably make noise the entire drive home.

Peter doesn't say anything.

I put my suitcase in the trunk. Part of the pet vacuum is sticking out the side.

Peter touches it and looks at me for explanation.

"For the cat hair," I say.

He nods.

I slide into the front seat next to Peter. I hold his sunglasses in case he needs them.

"Go," I say urgently.

He sets the GPS and turns the key in the ignition.

Sara is sick.

We need to get home.

That's all that matters.

I don't understand why Peter looks so happy.

Pandemic Phase Three (November 2020 through March 2021)

Chapter Twenty-Five

For kindness begins where necessity ends.
–Amor Towles, *The Lincoln Highway*

I am travelling.

This is not the way I usually travel. To somewhere far more interesting.

I am travelling back home with my husband. In a car.

I am surrounded by leather.

We are not alone in this car. My cat Chaos is strapped in the back seat.

Her only occupation is to make as much noise as possible while we drive.

We are on the road for two days and one night. During this time, October ends, and November begins.

There is no Halloween celebration, thanks to the virus. There are no pumpkins or decorations to mark the end of fall.

The trees look sad and brown as if coronavirus made them sick, too.

We can't stop and take a break at an interesting place along the way, because my daughter is sick.

It's urgent that we get home as soon as possible.

Nevertheless, Peter is a very slow and careful driver.

Several times over these two days, I threaten to kill him unless he lets me take control of the wheel and drive faster than fifty miles an hour on a highway.

While I'm driving, he doesn't say anything, but he has a death grip on the grab handle of the leather upholstered car door.

I admit that travelling with Chaos slows us down a bit.

There are not that many pet-friendly places to stay between Bryn Mawr, Pennsylvania and home.

Also, Peter has very high standards about where we stay. He is terrified about getting sick.

In the hotel lobby, he wears one mask on top of another and looks as grim as a career criminal.

When we get into our room for the night, though, he takes the masks off and sets up a litterbox for Chaos. He places food and water in the opposite corner of the room.

I guess that's thoughtful. Since I can tell Peter is not a cat person in general.

Or a fan of Chaos in particular.

Chaos hides under the bed for the night. When Peter sees there's no way she's coming out, he puts the litterbox under the bed, too.

I hope Chaos uses it.

The bed situation is awkward. Peter has paid for a large room with a couch and a king bed.

I don't sleep well in hotels. The noise of the heater or the air conditioner bothers me.

I tell Peter that I will sleep on the couch. As I won't sleep well, anyway.

But Peter says no. He puts my suitcase over by the bed and lies down on the couch himself. He says goodnight politely and turns his head to the wall.

I can stare at him, but he can't see me.

Maybe he wants to be as far away from Chaos as possible.

Or maybe he wants to be as far away from me as possible. I've been away a long time. I'm sure Peter suspects that I've been sleeping with someone else.

I'm not going to tell him the details. I might never tell him. Because why cause unnecessary pain?

Of course, maybe I should have thought of that before I left.

I lie awake thinking about Yonatan and feeling guilty. Wishing I had made different choices.

I get out of bed and take a long shower. All my muscles ache.

I dry my hair and get into bed. Peter has set himself up on the couch and is reading from his Kindle.

"Oh, for God's sake," I say. "Just get into bed with me. Maybe if you get some sleep, you won't drive like such an old man tomorrow."

Peter looks surprised, but he doesn't argue. He gets under the covers.

He is wearing a pair of flannel pajamas that I bought him for his birthday.

He is warm and, I admit, comforting curled up around me. I sleep.

In the morning, when we wake up, Chaos is in the bed lying between us, purring. Her cat food and water are gone.

I order room service because I don't want to eat in a restaurant and leave Chaos all alone in the room.

Peter is happy with this arrangement. He thinks in the restaurant all the customers are passing germs back and forth.

I let Chaos sit on my lap during breakfast and lick my plate.

I wouldn't allow this at home, but I do enjoy seeing Peter look queasy.

He doesn't say anything, though.

It has become Peter's job to engineer Chaos in and out of the travelling crate, and he is trying to get Chaos to like him.

His plan isn't working very well, though. I see Chaos scratch and bite him, but he doesn't complain.

He gets Brownie points from me for this.

Of course, I could crate and uncrate Chaos with no problems, but I want her to get used to Peter. And Peter to get used to Chaos.

Peter brings snacks for us to eat in the car from the buffet downstairs in the lobby.

He brings me two cups of coffee, a croissant, and a copy of the local paper. He even has some tuna fish and a little bit of cream cheese for Chaos.

She snarls at him when he puts it through the bars of her crate, but after a few minutes, her food is gone.

The second full day of driving, however, is even worse than the first day.

Before we leave, Peter buys a pair of earplugs in the hotel gift store. He can still hear Chaos protesting, but at least the sound is muffled.

He offers me a pair, but I shake my head. After all, she's my cat.

There are no good views of mountains or valleys to distract me from the road. Or the noise.

There are no pumpkins or apples or decorations to mark the end of fall.

When Peter drives, he's so slow I feel as if we're on a hamster wheel going around and around and never getting anywhere.

We take short breaks every few hours because Peter is convinced that if we don't get out of the car, we'll develop deep vein thrombosis.

I force him to let me drive for a while so we can actually make progress.

I persuade Peter to take a nap so I can drive much faster than he likes.

I'm stiff and sore from so many hours of sitting in the car. And tired of hearing Chaos's caustic comments on Peter's driving.

Even though he deserves them.

I just want to get home.

I recognize the scenery now and I don't even need to follow the directions on the GPS.

When I pull into our driveway, Peter wakes up. Suddenly, he looks nervous.

I look at him. "Did you forget to tell me something,

Peter?" I ask sweetly.

I hear barking inside the house. It sounds like a dog trying to make the loudest barbaric noise possible in hopes of winning a Guinness World Record.

In response, Chaos snarls and hisses inside her travelling crate.

"Oh right, that's Oskar," Peter says, not meeting my eyes. "You'll love him. He's Sara's best friend."

Of course he is. Peter is bringing Sara up to be a dog person.

Maybe it's good I'm back.

But what other changes did Peter make while I was away? Well, here's one.

The old lady I saw in the photographs comes to the door. She's wearing a mask. And holding Sara.

I plan to be aloof. To let this Mrs. Danvers know right away that I am Rebecca, mistress of Manderly.

I want her to be afraid of me.

I reach for Sara.

But Sara doesn't want me to hold her. She looks frightened and shrinks back.

I know this is normal behavior. Sara is old enough now to feel separation anxiety. She hasn't seen me for months. I'm a stranger. And she's sick. I can hear how congested she is, and I can see she is flushed with fever.

But it hurts that Sara doesn't leap into my arms.

It makes me feel like a bad mother. The kind of mother who would walk out the door and leave her daughter and husband because she wasn't strong enough to live the right way and teach her daughter the right things to do.

But before I can turn away, the old lady whispers something to Sara that makes her smile. She pops something in Sara's mouth to distract her. Then she puts Sara in my arms and says, "La tua bellisima bambina."

And now I'm totally disarmed.

Because Sara is beautiful. Although she looks exactly like me.

She's sick right now. But I can tell that when she's well, Sara is strong and happy and confident.

Was I once this way?

I know a little bit of Italian from travelling. "Molte grazie," I tell the old lady, and she nods.

"Alessia, per favore, incontratevi Sonia, la mamma. Sonia, please meet Alessia, our nanny," Peter says behind me.

Show off.

Peter is carrying Chaos in her crate in one hand, and he has our suitcases in his other hand. I can hear desperate barking coming from behind the closed door of the downstairs bathroom.

"Peter," I say, "please don't let Chaos out of her crate yet. Put her in the middle of the living room. Let Oskar sniff her while she's still in the crate."

Peter is more than willing to deposit Chaos on the living room rug. Not too close to the very expensive leather sofa and chairs.

I hope Oskar doesn't knock the crate over and eat Chaos.

When Alessia opens the bathroom door, a monster covered in curly brown fur shoots out.

Oh, no.

He skids on the floor and lands in front of Chaos's crate. There is a moment of silence while they sniff each other.

I can see Chaos bristling inside the crate, but Oskar wags his tail and lies down in front of the crate, belly up.

Then Oskar's attention switches first to Peter and then to me. He tries to knock Peter off his feet so he can cover him with saliva.

"Seduto, Oskar," Alessia says, and immediately Oskar sits.

Is it the tone of her voice, or is Oskar a bilingual dog?

Trilingual, actually, because he definitely barks dog language.

Sara is wiggling in my arms, trying to reach Oskar. I let her pet him and he trembles with desire to jump all over both of us but remains seated.

I do admire Oskar's beseeching brown eyes. And his soft touch ears.

Although I doubt Chaos will be a fan.

"Well, this is unexpected," I say to Peter. But I can't really concentrate on anything but Sara.

She doesn't seem afraid of me anymore. In fact, she seems very happy in my arms. She's already pulled my braid loose and drooled on my shirt.

I'm not sure I'll ever be able to put her down.

Sara is alert and smiling, but the nurse part of me notices that she feels warm and is breathing through her mouth. She's very congested.

"Alessia, is Sara's fever down?" Peter asks. Alessia shakes her head.

"Trouble breathing," she says, and I start to panic.

But I keep my voice calm.

"Let's get Sara something to drink," I say. "We'll check her temperature in a few minutes.

"And Peter, will you fill the humidifier in the nursery? Also, get the bulb syringe so I can suction out some mucus and make her more comfortable."

Peter is happy to obey me. Oskar follows him as he goes upstairs to the nursery.

Alessia goes into the kitchen and comes back with a sippy cup of water for Sara.

So far, so good.

I remind myself that I'm here to get Sara back to health.

After that, we'll see what happens. What all this means for travelling.

But right now, I don't want to go anywhere.

I'm not sure I'll ever be able to put Sara down.

Chapter Twenty-Six

Like an ouroboros eating itself over and over again, we
come back upon ourselves doing the same things in different ways, different settings for the same old scenes.
    –Donal Ryan, *Heart, Be at Peace*

Sara and I travel on the same path together.
    For several days, we cover the same route over and
over.
    Categorically I refuse to take my daughter where this jour-
ney leads.
    Instead, our travel is circular.
    Back and forth from the nursery to the living room to the
kitchen to the bedroom to the bathroom.
    Carrying Sara. Putting her down. Picking her up. Taking
her temperature.
    Changing her diaper. Trying to get her to drink. Trying to
get her to eat. Trying to get her to sleep.
    Cleaning her vomit. Changing her clothes. Cleaning and

refilling the humidifier.

Chaos makes herself scarce. I think she's spending most of her time sleeping in one of the kitchen cupboards where Oskar can't reach her.

Oskar follows me around everywhere, trying to get Sara to respond to him.

Alessia doesn't follow me around, but she is always there.

Sometimes I need the thermometer, or I need Alessia to hold Sara so I can listen to her lungs.

I am grateful for Alessia's help. I don't ask her to cook or clean but she makes all our food and scrubs every surface in the house.

I live on coffee. I can't eat while Sara is vomiting. I can't sleep while she is crying.

Peter is a doctor, and I am a nurse, and nothing we do is working.

Peter thinks Sara has coronavirus. I don't.

Peter goes to the hospital, brings tests home, and brings them back to the hospital to be deciphered.

This is taking professional courtesy too far, but he would break any rule and abuse any privilege he has for Sara.

All the tests for the virus are negative.

I try to figure out why Sara is so sick.

Has she been in contact with anyone besides Peter and Alessia?

Have any other adults been in the house?

I would love to blame this sickness on my parents, but they were here so long ago even I admit it's unlikely Sara picked these germs up from them.

Peter says that his friend Colin comes over every week. Oskar has a playdate with Colin's dog. They enjoy running around together.

Colin brings his children, so everyone plays outside. Peter grills food and Alessia supplies drinks and desserts.

There is a picnic in our backyard. A reminder of the world before the virus.

Everyone eats outside, but they run inside repeatedly to use the bathroom or get a glass of water or change Sara's diaper or borrow some of her toys.

Colin's children are a bit older than Sara. They wear masks, but not gloves.

Sara touches everything and puts her hands in her mouth.

Maybe Colin's children are sick and don't know it and leave virus or bacteria in our yard or in our house.

Maybe the carrier is Colin. Or Alessia. Or Peter.

Maybe Oskar carries germs in from outside.

Or maybe this sickness is something entirely different.

Environmental. Genetic even.

Unlikely. But I can't figure out the root cause.

When your child is sick, lying to yourself becomes necessary.

Every time Sara's temperature drops a degree or so, I can see the relief in Peter's eyes.

When Alessia coaxes her to eat a little, we smile.

When Sara falls asleep in my arms, I tell myself that she is improving.

There is no wheezing. I tell myself how fortunate we are to have no history of asthma. Not on Peter's side and not on my side of the family.

But with symptoms of asthma, at least I would know what to do and Sara would recover.

Every tiny step toward health is exaggerated. Setbacks are minimized.

Until it's clear that our feelings, no matter how intense, cannot change this trajectory.

We do everything we can. But after a few days, even Peter sees that nothing we do is enough.

Sara has to go to the hospital. She's having too much trouble breathing.

I think Sara may have pneumonia.

Or coronavirus, of course, but I think she has pneumonia. Maybe caused by respiratory syncytial virus or coronavirus.

Remember Jim Henson? So talented, someone I admire from afar.

I still miss him. I felt so cheated when he died.

Jim Henson is the poster child for "do not wait too long to start treatment for pneumonia."

I will not wait too long with Sara.

If whatever is in her lungs travels into her bloodstream, she can become septic.

The best place for her now is the intensive care unit.

The problem is, if Sara is admitted, Peter and I will not be allowed to stay with her.

Whether or not she has coronavirus.

She'll be all alone.

Peter is terrified.

He suggests silly things like putting sugar in her water

bottle to get Sara to drink more.

He begs for more time at home. Because the hospital is so dangerous right now.

I understand how Peter feels, but we don't have a choice.

Alessia and I don't pay any attention to him.

We're not friends yet, but we don't have time to be enemies.

We're united on this.

Peter offers to bring home a portable x-ray machine to help figure out exactly what is in Sara's lungs.

"We don't have enough time," I tell him. Not to mention that Peter can get fired for this. It is totally against the rules.

Peter doesn't care if he gets fired.

I tell him he can read the x-rays once we get to the hospital, but that's all.

Alessia and I will do everything else.

We put Oskar in his crate with plenty of food and water. We wrap Sara up and put her into her car seat.

Alessia tries to get Sara to play with some of the baby toys in the car, but she can't.

Sara has no energy left over for anything except breathing right now.

And that's why we can't wait any longer.

Alessia buckles herself in next to Sara, and I get in the driver's seat. Peter sits next to me.

He holds my sunglasses.

I drive fast. There is very little traffic which is just as well because I am driving as if I am blaring a siren on an ambulance.

Nobody says anything.

Peter calls ahead so everyone knows we are coming in. They are waiting for us outside the hospital doors with a gurney.

It's funny the things you notice when you are in extremity. In fear for someone other than yourself.

The sounds of the birds in the background.

How the air feels unusually still and cold.

How everyone is wearing a mask except for Sara.

She is the only one who looks human.

Sara is rushed to the emergency room.

Only one parent is allowed to accompany her. Because of coronavirus.

I go with Sara. Peter and Alessia must wait.

I do not look back, but I hear Peter crying.

This is no time to indulge our emotions.

We must be competent.

I do not have privileges at this hospital, and even if I did, for ethical reasons, parents cannot work on their own children.

But I can watch and make sure the doctors and nurses do the right things.

The things that I would do.

And they do.

They check Sara's oxygen saturation with a finger oximeter. It's less than ninety percent, so they gently suction the mucus out of her nose before giving Sara oxygen through nasal prongs.

They take Sara's vital signs. I tell them the time I gave her acetaminophen this morning (less than two hours ago).

Sara still has a high fever. Even more worrying, she is lethargic.

A portable x-ray machine is brought to her bed. They take the scans to Peter to confirm the diagnosis.

Professional courtesy.

But at least now we know that Sara has pneumonia.

If she wasn't so sick, knowing this would make me feel better.

But no one jumps up and down with relief about pneumonia.

They ask me if Sara has any allergies to antibiotics. She doesn't that I know of.

I text Peter to be sure, and he confirms it.

They start an intravenous infusion. Sara doesn't react when they have a hard time finding her vein and have to stab her three times.

I wince for her.

I know I should be thankful we have a diagnosis. Now Sara will be given appropriate treatment. And she should respond.

But now comes the hard part.

Sara will be admitted and kept in the pediatric intensive care unit for the next two days. At least that long.

Until we find out if the antibiotics are working.

I am not allowed to go to intensive care with her.

Because of coronavirus.

I understand, but that doesn't make following the rules easier.

On a typical day, I could wait hours in the emergency room

while they struggle to find a bed for Sara.

But because of coronavirus, all elective procedures are canceled, and there is a bed available.

I don't want to leave her. I don't have a choice.

I am not allowed to kiss her, but I sing her a song until they wheel her onto the elevator.

One of the nurses leads me outside.

I'm given a telephone number so I can call to check on Sara.

And now I have to find Peter and Alessia so we can go home.

They are numb. As am I.

No one should ever have to bring a child to the hospital and leave without her.

Chapter Twenty-Seven

The chestnut avenue opened into a road, smooth but
narrow, which led into the untouched country.
–E.M. Forster, *Howard's End*

There are 195 different countries in the world.

I want to travel to all of them.

An almost unlimited number of destinations.

Someday, maybe, this number will increase because space travel will be accessible to everyone.

If that is so, I will become one of the first to explore new planets and new stars.

But for now, there are some destinations that call out to me personally, here, on this earth, just waiting for me.

Cat Island in Japan.

I must pet all the cats living there and make an offering at the shrine. How could I not? How could anyone not? (Except maybe dog people like Peter).

The Dead Sea in Jordan.

The water is so salty, it will hold me up. I'm not a good swimmer and I need some extra help from this geographic anomaly.

The Rainbow Mountain in Peru. Well, you get the brightly hued picture.

Except I am not going anywhere.

I discover that when your heart is surgically removed from your body, it is impossible to travel.

During these next few days, I barely move from the sofa in the living room.

I'm afraid to go into the nursery. I don't want to see if the toys come out at night, looking for Sara to find out why she isn't playing with them.

I can't escape how quiet the house is. Chaos and Oskar know Sara is missing.

They muffle their meows and barks.

Oskar sits on my feet to make me feel better.

Chaos licks my ears when she wants me to feed her.

Peter calls the hospital once an hour until one of his friends calls back and tells him to stop. He's pissing everyone off.

His friend promises that he will call us if there is any change.

But we don't hear anything. I sit with my phone in front of me, waiting.

I find out that under stress, Peter is a pacer, not a sitter.

He's also a runner. He tells me he started running after I left.

Now Peter covers five miles every morning, coming back with his shirt soaked and his eyes glassy. I picture him checking his phone to see if there are any messages about Sara as he ticks off every mile.

Alessia is the only person in the house who seems normal. She continues cooking and cleaning. She does not ask me about Sara. But I know she thinks about her.

I can't think about anyone else.

I get an email from Steph at the Center. I want to open it and respond to her, but I can't.

I know she's probably wondering when I will be back.

If I'm ever coming back.

I know I should at least answer Steph's email and tell her that my daughter is hospitalized.

All I have to do is explain. She will give me the time I need.

But I don't have the energy to start a conversation that isn't about Sara coming home.

It's not that I don't missing seeing everyone at the Center on weekends.

It's just that right now, it feels like a world away.

A universe away.

Where there is no Sara, there is no Sonia.

Halfheartedly I wonder if there is an emergency. Did a child or staff member catch coronavirus? Is the Center shut down?

Steph will email me if that happens. Right?

Or maybe she already did.

In a way, working at the Center is the ultimate travel destination for me. The place where Peter and Sara don't exist for hours at a time.

While I'm at the Center, I concentrate on the children in

front of me. Not on a child waiting for me at home.

But now everything has changed. I can't get into my car. I can't even get on my feet.

I am chained to the sofa and my phone. Waiting for Sara. Instead of Sara waiting for me.

Now I know how Peter must have felt when I left and he had no idea when, if ever, I would come home.

I will never make him feel like this again. Now that I know what it's like.

All I want is for the phone to ring.

To be summoned to the hospital to take Sara home.

At some point, while we're waiting, I go upstairs to Peter's office where he is sitting at his desk not even pretending to try to work.

I kiss the back of his head because I am so sorry I put him through this same feeling of hopelessness.

He grabs my hand.

We don't say anything, but he knows what I want to tell him.

I lean against him in the chair, and we don't move for a long time.

And then Peter's phone rings.

For a second, we freeze in place like human popsicles. We're afraid to answer.

Before Peter moves, I think of catastrophes that could be occurring right now on the other end of the line.

The hospital is on fire. The hospital has to evacuate because of a bomb threat.

There is an active shooter in the hospital. A plane has fallen on the hospital and the ICU is crushed.

Sara has a bad reaction to the antibiotics. She's getting worse and we need to come right away. She's septic.

No.

I won't think of *all* the possible catastrophes. Some are un-thinkable.

Peter answers the phone, giving me time to get hold of myself and feel angry that the hospital called him instead of me.

Oh, yes, it's much better to feel angry than to keep thinking.

Peter never hits the right button for the speaker, so I don't even know what is going on.

"We'll be there right away," he says. And he hangs up.

He looks at me.

"We can take her home," he says.

I'm speechless.

I know that antibiotics work for other children.

I wasn't sure they would work for my child.

Because I'm so different. A traveller.

It seems Sara is a more normal person than I am.

Or maybe I'm not so different after all.

In less than fifteen minutes we are in the car on the way to the hospital.

"Ordinarily they would keep her a few days longer, just to be safe," Peter says as I drive. "But she's responding to the antibiotics. Because of the virus, they think she'll be better off at home."

She'll be with us. So yes, of course Sara will be better off at home.

"They warned me she's very cranky," Peter says. We both smile. Crankiness is a good sign. It means Sara is getting better.

As usual, getting discharged from the hospital takes four times as long as getting admitted. But we are abnormally happy and free of frustration despite all the missteps.

Sara's discharge papers aren't signed. So what? We are patient. We don't yell at anyone.

Peter goes to pick up Sara's meds at the pharmacy, and finds they are not ready. He hums while he waits.

I'm fine with however long it takes to get the paperwork signed because the hospital lets me hold Sara.

Well.

I mean, I am supposed to wait in the lobby but that's never going to happen.

I have no interest in obeying the rules the way I did three days ago when we left Sara here.

This is me, Sara's mother, coming to pick up my child.

I find out the room she is in right away.

I go there and pick her up out of her hospital bed and hold her and no, I am not putting her down. Even if someone asks me to.

Sara is howling and miserable.

Great. This is great. No, really.

So much better to see her this way than limp and lethargic.

I may never put her down again.

I do put Sara in the car seat when they finally let us though the hospital doors. I sit next to her in the back, and I am happy to let Peter drive.

I know he will be very careful.

I tell Sara we're travelling home to Alessia and Oskar and Chaos.

Travel. Home. Family. All together.

Is this really me? Am I the same person I was six months ago?

Am I a good person?

Am I a sane person?

I don't know. I don't care.

I am a *grateful* person.

I have Sara in my arms, and I may never put her down again.

Chapter Twenty-Eight

This air which I do not know is also a prayer, an entreaty
to happiness not to be too cruel, a bowing of the head
and as it were a falling on the knees before happiness…
–Alain Fournier, *The Wanderer*

I want to travel to Lone Wolf, Oklahoma.

Not just because it has the most beautiful name.

Finally, my travel exile may come to an end.

Finally, according to the news, a vaccine is coming.

A vaccine can make it safe to live like a human being instead of a creature hunted by coronavirus.

At least, I hope so.

Because Peter and I work in healthcare, we may be among the first to receive the vaccine. Peter is trying to figure out a way for Alessia to get it, too.

Sara is too young to be vaccinated. It will take a while before the vaccine is approved for infants. But I will feel much better knowing the people around her have a better chance to stay healthy and keep her healthy.

I can't go through coming back here and finding Sara sick again. The experience is like having brain surgery.

Absolutely nothing else matters except getting Sara to recover and making sure she is in the best possible environment to be well. And now, keeping Sara well is my top priority.

We will not hop into a travel vehicle when we get the vaccine. We will wait the full period to make sure we are fully immunized.

But once people are vaccinated, we can leave our houses.

Just going shopping will feel like a luxurious vacation.

A real vacation, where we leave our house and sleep somewhere else during the night, will feel like a trip to the moon.

I want to take Sara on a real vacation.

I think I can persuade Peter to rent a recreational vehicle next year. Sara will be almost two years old by then, and ready to travel with us. We can take her camping in Quartz Mountain State Park in Lone Wolf, Oklahoma.

I wonder if we will see a lone wolf when we get there.

I think I used to be a lone wolf, but I am not one anymore.

If Peter agrees to travelling in an RV, we'll have plenty of room for all four of us. I would not want to go on vacation without Alessia. I respect her more than I like her, but I listen to her when we have different points of view about Sara. She knows so much.

I do not want Alessia to go back to Italy. Also, I do not want her to want to go back to Italy. I think Sara is lucky to have her as almost a surrogate grandmother.

Peter will insist that we talk to Alessia and give her the

freedom to go back, though. If she wants to.

But if Alessia is there, that means I can put a small amount of time aside just to spend with Peter. He deserves that.

We might visit the mid-century lodge in the Park. The lodge was built during the time of Franklin Delano Roosevelt. I want to explore all the buildings in the Park, although I doubt this one is kid friendly. There's a restaurant, but I will understand if the wait staff prefer older children to toddlers with sticky hands.

If we're in an RV, we can bring our own baby food and supplement with local treats. I think Sara would like to go hiking with us. Or I can let her run around in the meadows and pick wildflowers.

For Peter, there is a golf course. Although golf is so boring I am not sure Peter plays it. He's better than that, I think.

We will have to find a cat sitter for Chaos, but we might bring Oskar on our trip. That would make Sara happy. Alessia not so much.

I think about our summer vacation while I sit in the back-yard with Sara, Alessia and Oskar.

Sit is the wrong word, because sitting with Sara means walking two steps behind her on full alert in case she picks something up from the grass and eats it. Or loses her balance and falls against a hard part of the playground.

Sara is recovered from her pneumonia now. I try not to be overprotective, but it's hard. She is well enough and strong enough now so she can walk up to the patio window. She doesn't yet understand why she can't kiss Chaos through the glass.

Alessia clicks her tongue at me for letting Sara smear the glass with her dirty hands, but I want Sara to know it's okay to get dirty when you're outside.

Chaos is an indoor cat; she does not go out and she spits at Oskar when he catapults himself inside from the yard. But Chaos is sitting watching Sara on the other side of the patio door. She has reservations about Sara grabbing her by the tail, but I think she's purring.

I want to teach Sara to be a cat person. She's already a dog person, and I won't take that away from her. But I want her to know how honored she will be if Chaos decides to be her friend.

Alessia is letting me take a turn on Sara alert so she can work in the garden. We have so many fresh vegetables now, we can't eat them all.

Peter suggested buying another freezer, but Alessia will not agree to this. Alessia is canning to preserve as much of the garden as possible for the winter. She is teaching me to do it, too.

Someday, I will teach Sara how to do it. And this summer, we can take some of these vegetables with us in the RV.

I can't persuade Peter to rent the RV yet because right now, he is upstairs on a Zoom meeting with his colleagues at the hospital.

This time, travelling will be different.

I hope Peter will want to travel with me. With all of us as a family.

But I'm worried because the last time we went on a trip together, I was not very nice to him.

When I travelled with Peter, I thought I was seeing everything through his eyes. I thought he was trying to control me.

I don't think that anymore.

Now, travelling is about seeing the world through my own eyes. *And* Peter's eyes. *And* Sara's eyes. All the different perspectives, together.

I want to show Sara everything. And help her understand what she is seeing.

A mountain. A river. A meadow of wildflowers.

All new.

I want Peter to enjoy all this, too. And to enjoy it in person, not by looking through a camera.

Although if he insists on doing that, I will let him. After what we just went through at the hospital, I do understand why he wants to document every second of Sara's life.

There is something else I have to ask Peter, and it won't be as easy as asking him to rent the RV.

I have to ask him about our future.

Here, in the sunny yard, with Sara learning to walk, and Oskar chewing on his rope toy, life seems so safe and sheltered.

But I can't take refuge here forever.

There are children who need me at the Center.

I want to stay here with Sara for most of the week. I want to be part of her growing up.

But I still want to work at the Center on weekends.

With Alessia here, this seems more and more possible.

Only I wish we didn't live so far away. I won't be able to drive there. Peter will have to agree to me taking the train.

It will be safe to take the train once everyone is vaccinated.

Or I could fly, but I think I would do that only if there is an emergency.

And I would have to keep my apartment. Even though it won't feel the same without Chaos living there with me.

I will have to keep my tiny rental car, too. There's no way Peter will ever agree to keeping one of the cars we own outside in a parking space instead of a garage.

How will Peter feel about all this? Will he think I am trying to leave again?

Because I'm not.

He might ask me to try to find a job working with disabled children somewhere closer to home, so I don't have to be away all weekend.

I don't want to do that.

I want to be with Gulie and Jeff and Louise and Thomas and the other children at the Center.

I want to know if the person who hurt Jeff has been arrested.

I want to make sure all the children are taking their meds.

I hope Peter will understand that this time, travelling to the Center isn't travelling away from our family.

It's my way of travelling toward all of us instead.

Not the way it was before.

This time, I won't feel trapped. I won't feel that I have to run away to be myself.

I feel myself most now when I'm with Sara. And Peter.

I'll miss them while I'm away.

But I'll appreciate them even more when I come back.

Chapter Twenty-Nine

That was all that ever came between us, Clarissa thinks—the Great Wall of China. –Elizabeth Tallent, *Museum Pieces*

The backyard is a good place to dream about travelling. But after a few hours, Sara starts to get restless. We travel back inside the house, a place where daydreams about the future seem a little impractical.

The house is so now. So Peter.

Definitely not me. But yes, quite a bit Sara. So, I can't hate it.

Alessia takes Sara from me and puts her on her hip. She goes into the kitchen to start dinner.

This is how we usually spend the early evening; with Alessia teaching Sara how to cook and with me free to read or spend some time with Peter.

Tonight, I need to change things.

I go upstairs and very quietly open the door of Peter's study. He's not on Zoom anymore, just making notes on the computer for the week's assignments.

"I need you after dinner tonight," I tell him. "I want to talk about the summer."

Peter nods, not really paying attention to me.

"And a few other things," I add. "You'll see."

Peter is too engaged with the computer to become apprehensive.

I go downstairs and take out my favorite gastronomic book. I used to like to cook, before Alessia came. I have a box full of collected recipes.

Alessia watches with a contemptuous expression. She never needs to use a recipe.

"Alessia, please will you let me take over in the kitchen tonight?" I ask. "I want to make something special for Peter."

Alessia looks at me skeptically. "Lei sa cucinare?" she says.

I'm pretty sure she's asking me if I know how to cook, and I nod.

"It's just for tonight," I clarify. "I have a favorite recipe I want to use."

I might as well ask for Alessia to strip naked and teach Sara how to pole dance. I'm sorry, Alessia.

She glares at me and takes Sara to the nursery, Oskar trailing behind as usual.

Chaos, however, looks interested and arranges herself neatly on one of the stools around the island. I know Alessia would swat her off, but I let her sit there.

I have a few recipes that Peter really likes. I haven't made them for him in a long time.

One, that is very quick, is cornbread. Alessia thinks

cornbread is barbaric, but Peter and I like it. Chaos likes it because one of the ingredients is milk.

Chaos always knows what I am doing before I do.

Another very simple recipe is a stir-fry; made with whatever vegetables I have on hand. Tonight, it's mushrooms, spinach and eggplant from Alessia's garden.

In honor of Alessia, I mince some garlic and grate some cheese on top.

I know my cooking is anticlimactic compared to Alessia's cooking, but I hope Peter will still like this special dinner.

Finally, I make Peter a small apple and blueberry crumble. There's a secret ingredient in the crispy oat topping that gives it extra flavor. It's granulated maple syrup.

Alessia doesn't have a clue what's in the crumble, so she would never try to make it. Her cooking is sublime, anyway. Mine is occasionally good.

But my cooking may have nostalgia for Peter that Alessia can never replicate.

At least, I hope so. For tonight.

And at first, the dinner goes very well. Peter is surprised and touched that I cooked.

"This is a nice change," he whispers, touching my foot under the table.

Everything tastes good. Even Alessia nods grudgingly when she samples the crumble. After dinner, Peter lets Sara watch a cartoon on the gigantic television in the den. Alessia and I put the dishes in the dishwasher. We wipe the counters.

Alessia waves me away. "Vai a parlare con tuo marito," she orders.

This is one of the few times when I wish Peter was more European. It would be nice if he drank a reasonable amount wine on a regular basis. Just to get him to relax a bit.

But Peter is way too Puritanical to enjoy wine. He drinks only on social occasions.

Nevertheless, Peter already looks relaxed and happy to see me when I take Sara from him and give her to Alessia.

It's bathtime. Oskar barks. Chaos flees.

Lots of splashing and happy screaming from Sara.

Silence from Alessia, who has regained her habitual dour look.

I sink down on the leather couch next to Peter. I snuggle against his shoulder. I don't want him to think this is a shake-down.

Even though it is. Sort of.

Peter looks pleased.

I start by telling Peter how much fun it would be to take a real vacation during the summer. Our celebration of freedom, thanks to the vaccine.

And to my surprise, he's very receptive to this idea.

"We could take a whole week off," he says. "Or maybe even two weeks. I think Alessia will enjoy seeing a different part of the country."

So that's great. Something to look forward to.

But now to the hard part.

I try to explain to Peter how important it is for me to go back to working part time at the Center.

And right away his face tightens.

He thinks I am leaving him again.

I'm not. I have to make Peter understand.

I start by assuring him that Sara is now my main focus. I am on perpetual alert to make sure she stays well.

I'm not sure Peter believes me, but this is the truth.

"If you care so much about Sara, why do you want to leave again?" he asks. "You just got back. She's just getting used to you again."

I try to tell him how worried I am about the children at the Center. I describe each person I care about.

I have so many questions.

Is Gulie eating enough and drinking enough? Is she getting the attention she requires?

Is Thomas being stimulated enough? And loved enough?

Is Louise pretending she can't do her homework so one of the male aides pays attention to her?

Does Jeff know that the person who broke his arm is still working at the Center, but he's unable to reveal the predator's identity?

I explain the difficulty with Jeff to Peter and he is horrified.

"But why is this your problem?" he asks. "Why haven't they figured this out yet?"

I shrug.

"No one cares enough," I admit. "These kids are very low priority for the police. But I pay more attention than some of the others do. I think I can find out who it is if I go back."

"How do you not see how dangerous that is?" Peter demands. "The police should be working on this, not the staff."

"I know that," I say, reaching for his hand. "But Jeff can't be a witness. He can't fight back. I have to fight for him."

Peter shakes his head.

"It doesn't matter what I say. You're going to leave again," he says quietly. "At least you're telling me this time."

"It does matter," I argue. "I do care what you think. You're making me realize that I have to be very careful. But I can do this. And it's only for a couple of days a week."

He looks away.

"I would take the train on Friday night," I explain, watching his face. "And then I would take the train back Sunday night. That's only two nights a week away from home. I think you and Alessia can handle that."

As I talk, I wonder why I'm trying so hard to get Peter to agree. Do I really want to do this?

Once, working with the children at the Center felt like a vacation from real life. A place where everyone has the same noble goal of helping the children.

What a crock of shit.

Now, I'm afraid of finding out that the Center isn't the refuge I think it is. Instead, it might be a place where the children are in daily danger.

Because a predator is unpredictable.

Do I want to risk hurting Peter this way to go to such a place? Because I can tell he's hurt.

It would be so much easier to stay home. To behave the way everyone expects me to, as a wife and mother.

To stop being a traveller the way I used to be.

I'm not even totally sure I want to travel to the Center. Maybe I know it's not good for me anymore.

But if I stop working at the Center, will living here be

enough for me?

I don't think so.

I am not travelling back to be altruistic. I am travelling back to be selfish.

This is something I need, for myself.

"And what if Alessia goes back to Italy?" Peter asks. "What then?"

"Well, then," I say, "we reevaluate. Because I wouldn't feel comfortable leaving Sara with someone else."

Even though that's exactly what happened when I left the first time.

Both Peter and I are aware of the hypocrisy. He's kind enough not to call me on it.

"Can we compromise?" I ask.

I can tell Peter is surprised that I'm offering a compromise. Instead of an ultimatum.

"Can we try this for a month?" I ask. "After I get the vaccine, of course. So I don't bring virus back to our house."

I can see he is more open to this idea. To a time limit.

"I'm reading it will take some time for the vaccine to be fully protective," I add. "I'd have to wait until two weeks after the second dose."

We don't know exactly when the first dose of the vaccine will arrive at our hospital. Peter likes knowing that I won't leave right away. It gives him time to get used to the idea.

"That sounds more reasonable," he says cautiously. "And if it doesn't work out?"

I spread out my hands. "Then we reevaluate," I say. "The same way we do if Alessia leaves."

Neither of us know exactly what reevaluating means. I suspect to Peter, it means that if there is the slightest problem, we call the whole thing off.

"What if there's an emergency?" Peter argues. "Can I trust you to put Sara first?"

"Yes," I say. And I mean it. "If anything happens to Sara, you call me or text me or both and I'll come home on the next train. I promise I'll answer this time. We'll have a special signal word that means get back right now."

I can tell Peter is still against me working at the Center. He might even call me when Sara isn't sick just to see if I respond.

But I deserve that. I didn't put Sara's needs first last time.

I will now.

Peter gives in.

"I don't want to lose you again," he says. "So we'll try it. For a month."

I hug him.

I don't say thank you.

Because I shouldn't have to.

"You won't lose me," I tell him. "You might gain me."

And just like that, now travelling is real again.

I think I felt safer when it was imaginary.

Chapter Thirty

"Come to the Labyrinth," said Ash. "You'll be totally taken care of." –Meg Wolitzer, *The Interestings*

I'm on the train that is taking me to the Center.

It's my first trip travelling this way to work, and it's quite comfortable, but I'm nervous.

I miss Sara already. And Peter. I tell myself I'll see them in two days. After all, this trip was my idea, so I should be happy, right? But I'm not.

I've brought a book to keep myself busy until the train arrives. I prop my feet up on my duffel bag and try to read but I can't concentrate.

Robert Benchley said, "There are two kinds of travel: first class and with children." I don't agree! I think when you're travelling first class, you're more intent on all the luxuries you've paid for than the scenery passing by and the new experiences.

I want to take Sara everywhere. Economy class is fine. The

problem is, there are not a lot of planned vacations where babies and toddlers are encouraged. I may have to wait until Sara is older to take her on a trip other than in a recreational vehicle.

I'd like to take Sara on a train ride for families. Maybe something more adventurous as she gets older, but when she's six years old, the Chocolate Train in Switzerland sounds about right. I imagine Sara wearing a red beret and a blue duffel coat, standing between Peter and me. Waiting for the train and holding our hands. I see her jumping up and down with excitement.

Way before we get on the train, there's the excitement of travelling by air to Switzerland. Peter insists that we travel business class or at least premium economy, and I won't argue since this is Sara's first time on an airplane.

Just watching the different colors of the ground change as the plane gains altitude, then looking down at the clouds fascinates her. When that wears off, at judicious intervals I bring out special books and tiny toys to keep Sara occupied while we fly.

When we land in Switzerland, Peter and I take Sara straight to the hotel so she can sleep and recover from jet lag. And before we get on the Chocolate Train, Peter and I make sure Sara has a good breakfast of Swiss muesli and hot chocolate.

We also spend some time in the Musée de Montreux. It's a child-centric place where Sara can bake and make chocolate, or paint and play outside. Today, Sara is all about playing outside and meeting new friends.

Peter enjoys the Chocolate Train, because in addition to

Swiss chocolate, he gets to sample Swiss cheese (not surprisingly, the real kind is so much better than our supermarket brand).

Part of the trip involves visiting castles as well as cheese and chocolate factories. Peter loves taking pictures of architectural details. He'll take pictures inside a factory too, but he'll always choose to photograph a stone gargoyle rather than a metal lever.

Peter prefers travelling in a vintage Pullman car, but for Sara, I choose the panoramic coach car instead. She gets the window seat so she can see all the Swiss countryside as we travel from Montreux.

Peter looks longingly at the car with the fancy gold piping around the red cushions, but after a while, he's absorbed in looking out the window too.

Once we get to the Gruyère region, it's time to learn about cheese and chocolate. Everything to bring on a migraine headache. But Peter and Sara and I sample judiciously and buy a lot of presents to take back to our neighbors and friends and colleagues.

I assume Peter and I will be working when Sara is older. Peter won't feel threatened by me working at the Center by then. We will still be together. We will be happy and Alessia will be with us.

Although I don't see Alessia taking this trip to Switzerland. I'm afraid if we take her with us so close to Italy, she'll decide to return home.

It's selfish of me to deny her that opportunity. Maybe Alessia comes with us, and we give her a vacation in Italy.

And then she returns to our house to take care of Oskar and Chaos.

I imagine how miserable they'll feel if we put them in a kennel while we're away. But I can see Alessia bringing them home from the kennel and how happy they are to be home with her. And how relieved Alessia is to have some peace and quiet in our house with just Oskar and Chaos to take care of for a week.

I hope I am not making up my own fairy tale.

But now the conductor comes by to take my ticket and tell me to follow him to the middle of the train so I can get off at the correct stop for the Center.

Everything has become very real, very fast.

I text Peter so he knows I arrived safely. I don't want him to worry.

When I disembark from the train, it's only a short walk to my apartment. One of the nice things about living here is that I can hear the train from my bedroom, every two hours, and it's a comforting sound. When I first moved here, the train whistle woke me up, but now it's just part of my dreams.

As I walk, I look at the golden lights in the houses around my apartment building. This is my favorite color of light—it's so cozy and warm. Like firelight in a bulb.

I always thought I would be looking at these houses with golden lights from the outside, always walking by, never going inside. But now I have my own family inside a house with golden lights. I will be an insider again in just two days.

The apartment is just as I left it. My tiny car is still in my assigned parking space.

I'm glad I had the foresight to empty out the refrigerator (there wasn't much in it) and take the garbage out before I left.

I've been away much longer than I thought I would. It feels strange to turn on the lights and turn up the heat, because now it is almost December and the air is cold, although not unfriendly.

I do miss Chaos. Usually before bed, she sits in my lap and purrs to help me feel sleepy. I can tell I will want to go home as soon as my shifts are over, so I can pet her and Oskar. He is not such a terrible dog after all.

And, of course, I need to hug Sara and Peter.

I call home in the morning before I go to work, to make sure everyone is surviving without me. And they are fine, Alessia tells me.

"Tourna a casa appena puoi," she orders.

"Domenica sera," I answer.

I enjoy the short drive to the Center in my no-frills car, where I can play my own music (Buffy Sainte-Marie) and not worry if I spill a little coffee on the upholstery. It's red pleather, and impervious to stains or blots.

And then, I'm at the Center, and right away, Gulie veers into me and I can see Louise turning her wheelchair away, so she doesn't have to say hello. I get down on my knees to hug Gulie, but she doesn't want to be touched today. Which is nothing unusual.

I think she's happy to see me, though.

Alessia gave me a big tin of cookies to bring to work, and these last all of five minutes after I arrive. It's pretty much hug a colleague, offer them a cookie, hear them gasp with appreciation, offer them another cookie, and tell them that I did enjoy my time off.

No one really wants to know what I have been doing, and no one is really listening, but they certainly pay attention to the cookies.

My first two days here are relatively easy. I get back into the habit of giving meds to the children and assessing their physical and emotional needs since I see all of them at least twice per shift.

I notice that it's much harder to get Jeff to take his meds than it used to be. He's a very hungry little boy, and it's been easy to put his meds inside a piece of cheese, so he gobbles them up.

Now though, he pushes me away. He's strong, but Jeff's not using his left arm much anymore, either. The cast is off, but when he plays with toys now, he's only using his right arm.

He's seeing a physical therapist twice a week and she gives us exercises to do with him in between visits. But it's hard to get him to do the exercises. He scoots himself away as soon as the aides touch him.

I talk to Steph and the other nurses about Jeff. We're all having the same problems getting him to take his meds, and we've all noticed that he's lost some weight.

I crush Jeff's meds up and put them inside a little vanilla ice cream with a lot of chocolate syrup. Jeff can't resist that. But we still have no idea who is responsible for breaking Jeff's arm.

I tell myself that because I've been away for a while, I'll figure out who did this. I will look at the people working here without any preconceptions.

But my entire month, four weekends, goes by without me even getting suspicious of anyone. Not even Martin, the new weird guy. And he was one of the most likely candidates.

Well, maybe that's not fair. But Martin is a little bit weird. And a little bit new.

I tell myself not to trust anyone. I watch all the aides just in case I've missed something.

But I don't see anything.

I see how tender Jenna is when she brushes Louise's hair. She does a gentler job than I do when she tugs out the snarls. I tend to get impatient because Louise moves her head so much.

Of course, it's unlikely that the person who is hurting Jeff is a woman. And even more unlikely that Jenna would be the one. But I give her the same attention I give everyone else. Just in case. Just to be fair.

I warn myself that the women who work here are as likely to act out against the children as the men. And they are as physically strong as the men. We don't have any bodybuilder types working here. Men or women.

In other words, it seems so unlikely that someone who works here is hurting a child. But I don't have any other reasonable explanation based on the date of Jeff's injury. There were no strangers logged into the Center that day. No doctors (they don't come that often). No physical therapists. Not even any parents.

I think whoever is doing this knows they're being watched, and is not doing it regularly. Not on any kind of a schedule.

That makes it harder to know what to look out for.

Louise's parents pay extra for her to see an occupational therapist twice a week, but that woman is over seventy years old and very frail. And she never goes near any of the children except for Louise.

I just don't think the occupational therapist has it in her to hurt anyone anyway. It's a miracle that she's gotten so close to Louise.

I watch Ben take Thomas for special field trips to see movies. Thomas is so quiet and so well-behaved in his wheelchair that he gets extra privileges.

I think about that, and I manage to make excuses to come along on two of these trips. Once we go to see a Marvel Universe movie in 3D. I think the movie is chosen more for Ben than for Thomas, but he seems to enjoy it too, especially the goggles.

Another time we take Thomas to an outdoor concert. Ben is very attentive, making sure that Thomas's wheelchair is in a good spot. He fusses over him being warm enough and he takes him to a diner for hot chocolate afterwards. I can't fault Ben's care at all.

Jeremy is quiet about it, but he likes taking care of Gulie. He brings her small brightly colored toys (too large to put in her mouth). She likes balls and soft plastic figures that she can squash, then watch them spring back up. Jeremy tries to get Gulie to roll a ball back to him, but so far, she has no interest in doing that. She lets the ball roll right to the other side of the room, screaming softly.

Gulie likes all the attention, though. She'll sit and play with Jeremy for longer periods of time than she ever spent with me.

I guess it's the guy thing. Gulie liked Yonatan, too. I wonder if she knows that Jeremy is a different person than Yonatan. I wonder if guys smell the same to her, or different.

Marta is the most senior of all the aides, so I'm not terribly worried about her. She's Jenna's cousin, too. She helped Jenna get a job here and taught her how to be an effective aide.

But just to be sure, I watch Marta patiently teaching Mandy to play a card game. Mandy doesn't get it—she'll never get it. Marta doesn't mind when Mandy knocks all the cards on the ground and laughs like an insane person. Marta just picks up the cards and tries to get Mandy to pay attention to the game.

I watch the nurses, too. It's even more unlikely that they would hurt a child, I tell myself. Because we, the nurses, have extra training and understanding that the aides don't have.

I know that's bullshit. Anyone can lose their temper. A doctor. A physical therapist. An aide. Even a nurse.

But I don't see anyone acting differently. Meena brings the children homemade candy on holidays. Steph tries to keep all of the nurses happy by making sure we all get our days off and no one feels aggrieved because of too much work.

There is not much nurse turnover at the Center. It's very different from the hospital. I thought I would miss rushing back and forth between the hospital and the Center, but I was wrong.

If I'm honest with myself, I don't want to go back to working full time. All the energy I poured into that hospital job is now going into my family instead.

I think it's because the hospital always feels like work. But the Center still feels like family.

Everyone who works with the children is doing a great job. At least, that's what I see.

I can't see everything. I can't be here twenty-four hours a day. There are other nurses and aides who work during the evenings and the nights. In some ways, it would make me feel better if the bad guy turned out to be someone that I don't know very well. Someone I see only for a short time during review before ending one shift and starting another.

And it is a bad guy. It must be.

Evening and night shifts are when the guys come out. More male aides, more male nurses. I'm not sure why they prefer the later shifts. Maybe they're out on a shooting range during the day getting ready for hunting season. Killing animals is a very popular activity in Pennsylvania.

While Jenna helps me clean out the med cart at night, I ask her if she knows any of the aides or nurses on the other shifts.

"No, not really," Jenna says. "I only see them in the parking lot."

Well, that makes sense.

But Jenna looks away, and I get the sense there's something she isn't telling me.

I keep my voice light.

"There are so many new guys since I started working part time. Did you ever date any of them?"

"Seriously?" Jenna snorts and I smile. Still, there's something.

"Have you spoken to any of them?"

Jenna looks away. "Only at the meetings where they try to get us to join a union, you know? There's a lot of unhappy people working here."

Now, that's news to me. But I haven't been to any of those meetings.

"What are they unhappy about?" I ask.

"Oh, the usual. We don't make enough money. We don't get enough overtime. Or holidays. We don't have really good benefits. There's no opportunity for advancement. That sort of thing."

I'm puzzled. We work for the state of Pennsylvania, and the benefits here are pretty good, I think. Much better than the aides could get at other jobs. After all, they're nice people but most of them stopped their education after high school.

"Is there something specific that everyone wants?" I ask.

Jenna glares at me. "Yes, specifically, it would be nice if the aides were allowed to work part time the way the nurses do. The way you do."

I feel guilty now.

We need aides who work full time because the children require continuity of care.

At least that's the story.

Nurses are allowed to work part time because our work is more specialized and more important. Or so we tell ourselves.

"Jenna, did you want to work part time?"

"No," Jenna says, "but I know other people who do. Not

everybody wants to spend their entire life here."

She walks away before I can find out more.

I feel as if I'm going around and around in circles. There's something that isn't right and it's so close to me, but I just can't reach it.

Like Jeff, I'm lost in my own labyrinth.

Neither of us are safe anymore.

Chapter Thirty-One

The insult of it happening in her own house—that was
what she could not swallow.
–Carson McCullers, *Reflections in a Golden Eye*

I t's a Saturday.

That used to be my favorite day of the week for travelling.

I'm in my little apartment. There's no soft and purring Chaos snuggled against my side. Waking up is harder without her paw on my cheek prompting me to start breakfast.

But even without Chaos, there's coffee to get me out of bed. I drink it with my legs stretched out in front of me on the sofa in the living room.

No one's awake yet except for me. I love being the first person to open all the doors of the morning.

Eventually, I will brush my teeth, take a shower, and get ready to go to work.

But first, I will travel. Just a short distance.

This trip that I take is my new Saturday morning ritual.

First, I imagine myself back at my home train station, surrounded by closed shops and benches full of tired families.

It's Sunday night, so all the commuters are home getting ready for the week to come.

As I've made my trips to the Center, I've learned that the people who frequent this train station on weekends are those who take their children for a brief visit to see relatives, maybe the ones they don't like very much. It's nice to have the excuse of having to go back to school and work on Monday to end the visit.

No one is here because they are returning from a supercharged job or because they think the train station is a glamorous place to hang out.

There's no distinctive history to this building or architectural value to photograph. It's just a necessary unpleasant taking-off point for busy lives.

Not especially clean. Not especially fun. No coffee or doughnuts for the kids on Sunday night. Even the newspaper store filled with unhealthy snacks is closed.

But I'm here, and because I'm returning from work, I'm happy.

I can't wait to get home. For me, the station is one step closer to home.

I have a small flashlight on my keychain, and I use it to find my other car in the train parking lot. It's not the car I rent in Pennsylvania. It's the one I shopped for with Peter because he's convinced car salespeople try to cheat women who come in by themselves to buy a car.

It's an eh, okay car. My Pennsylvania car is a lot more me, and a lot more fun to drive. Peter chose this car for safety reasons. I's loaded with every possible feature to prevent me from having an accident, alone or with Sara in the baby seat.

But I've been away for two days, so just seeing Sara's baby seat makes me happy. And when it's dark and windy and cold out, like tonight, I don't mind the heated seats and the extra-bright headlights. It's not such a terrible thing to feel secure while driving.

It's only a fifteen-minute drive home. There's not much traffic, and no construction to make me take another route and get lost.

I watch to make sure a baby squirrel or a cat doesn't try to cross in front of me. This car has excellent brakes, so I know I can stop short if I have to. But tonight, the drive is peaceful and quiet. In our town, the streets are bordered with many trees. On a windy night, the bare branches bend so far, the trees look as if they are talking to each other.

I press the garage door opener just before I get home so I can zip inside and close the door quickly. Peter hates for the garage door to stay open too long. He's afraid of chipmunks and squirrels getting in and destroying his expensive tools.

Not that that's ever happened.

And now I'm home.

The first thing I hear is Oskar's deep bark announcing my arrival. I go inside the house to pet him and shush him, so the barking stops before it wakes up the entire house. There's a lot of excited tail-wagging, but no more jumping. Peter has been taking Oskar to obedience classes, and finally, they're leading to a favorable effect on his behavior.

Chaos is curled up on the sofa waiting for me. One eye is open, so I know she's awake, but she's too comfortable to get up right now. I pet her behind the ears so I can hear her reflexive purr.

I tiptoe upstairs to Sara's room. She's asleep on her side, the blanket pushed down to the base of her crib. Soon she'll be too big for the crib, and I'll have to go on an interminable shopping trip with Peter to choose the very best, most lauded child bed.

Meanwhile, in her furry onesie, Sara is plenty warm enough without the blanket. But I cover her anyway and kiss her very lightly on her hair. She smells like watermelon.

Then I go into our room, where Peter is reading in bed, waiting for me.

I always tell him to go to sleep when I call before I get on the train, and he never does.

He wants to make sure that I get home safely. This doesn't irritate me anymore.

I kiss him and hang my travelling backpack on the hook on the back of the door.

"How was your weekend?" he whispers. "And the trip home?"

"All good," I whisper back. I grab my nightgown and go into our luxurious en suite bathroom to brush my teeth and get ready for bed.

It's only when I see myself in the mirror without my uniform on that I realize I'm home. And now I can spend another week with my family.

Now, I can sleep.

But this is just my fantasy for how the trip home will go tomorrow.

Reluctantly, I travel back into my tiny living room in Pennsylvania.

It's time to get ready for work at the Center.

Chapter Thirty-Two

Nothing so frightened Kazu as Yamazaki's prediction that
an emptiness would soon steal over her against which she
would not want to move a finger. When would it come?
–Yukio Mishima, *After the Banquet*
(translated by Donald Keene)

The day I find out the identity of the person who is
hurting Jeff starts out like any other ordinary day.
I drink coffee. I fantasize about returning home on
Sunday. I get ready for work.

I'm so glad this first month of commuting back and forth
is over. I'm not the kind of person who takes probation
lightly. I sweat every detail of this first month because I'm so
anxious to see if I can accomplish travelling back and forth to
work without messing up my commute, my job, or my family.

There are a few tense moments, but largely they are resolved…for now.

I can tell that Peter is just waiting for a train to be canceled or for me to be late getting off my shift so that I won't show up when I am supposed to.

But now that the month is over, even Peter admits that my new schedule of taking the train on Friday and coming back on Sunday is a success.

I mean, he doesn't say that, but he seems more relaxed about it. Not fighting me every step of the way.

Usually, when I get back, the first thing I do is to go into Sara's room to check on her while she's asleep. And because I completely focus on Sara and Peter during the week while I'm at home, I don't think they miss me too, too much over the weekends.

I miss them. And I miss Chaos. But I continue going to work. This job is important to me.

I have less housework in the apartment, because there's no cat food or cat hair to clean up anymore. I keep the refrigerator and pantry bare because it's just as easy to get coffee and food downtown or at work.

Alessia and Peter take care of the animals while I am away. Then I resume care when I get back.

My life starts to take on a pattern. A rhythm, a continuity.

I know what I'll be doing every day of the week. But I don't mind.

I used to think life is boring unless it is unpredictable. That's why I travel. But except for my weekly trips to work, and my weekly fantasies about going home, I don't seem to need so much travelling anymore.

Why would I spend time travelling when I have Sara?

I thought she didn't need me before. I was so wrong.

Sara is the center of surprise for me. She grows so fast.
Alessia and I can barely keep up.

When you are there for someone, really there, there is no need to travel.

I have so much to think about in my life. So much to do.

I am happy.

So, I almost don't notice what's happening one weekend while I am giving out meds at the Center.

Until Louise pinches me on my butt. Hard.

It really hurts.

"Ouch!"

I whirl around, keeping a hand on my med cart. We're taught to be careful of the meds at all times. To make sure no one unauthorized gets access to them.

It's not beyond the realm of possibility that Louise wants an extra snack with her meds. Is that why she pinched me?

Louise has brought her wheelchair right up behind me. I can see all her pimples and the drool on the side of her mouth. Her hair is shiny with grease. Her tiny eyes are blinking rapidly, and she is making the strange noises that mean she is trying to say something. With words that she never works hard enough to make clear for other people.

It's terrible to be a teenager and to be so ugly.

"Louise, please don't pinch me. Do you want some more applesauce?"

She knocks her wheelchair against me, pushing me in another direction.

"Louise, what is the matter with you? What are you doing?!"

She pushes me again, viciously. I'm going to have bruises on my leg from the wheelchair knocking into me.

I'm angry now. It feels as if Louise is attacking me.

And then, across the room, I see it.

Marta, one of the older aides who's been at the Center for years, is on the floor next to Jeff. She's doing his physical therapy exercises. Huge tears are coming out of Jeff's eyes.

I push my med cart across the room and come up behind Marta.

I can't believe what I'm seeing.

I see that Marta is the person who has been hurting Jeff.

Instead of moving his arm gently, she's pinching him.

And scratching him with her fingernails.

Not enough to leave marks, but enough to hurt.

Maybe Marta thinks Jeff is so strong he can't feel what she's doing to him?

But I look at her, and I'm shocked by the vindictiveness on her face.

I'm even more shocked because I've never seen this side of Marta before.

Or have I?

Have I seen this before? And I just didn't want to believe it?

Jeff is terrified. But he can't say anything.

"Marta, stop!" I scream. Loudly.

I scare her because she thinks I am across the room.

Marta looks up at me as if she's coming out of a dream.

Very quietly, so only I hear her, she says, "You cunt."

Jenna is the aide closest to me on the floor. She's helping

Thomas fingerpaint at the crafts table.

"Jenna, get Steph," I say urgently.

Jenna's eyes widen but she runs to the office behind the nursing station and comes back with Steph.

I see the weird new guy dash over to Jeff to comfort him.

"Marta and Sonia," Steph says. She looks very tired. "Let's go into my office, please."

"No," Marta says. "I haven't done anything wrong."

"Marta, you're hurting Jeff," I say. "Get away from him now."

Jenna is confused. She looks from me to Marta to Jeff.

"Sonia, what are you saying? Marta would never hurt anyone."

Marta points at me.

"Sonia's making up stories again," she says, her voice as deadly as a gun. "You can't trust her."

I'm so confused.

"What are you talking about, Marta?" Steph asks.

Marta hisses at me.

"*She's* the one who hurts people. Remember what she did to Yonatan? How she didn't even care about her husband and baby?"

I am in shock.

Not because Yonatan's name has been brought up.

Because Marta isn't admitting to what she just did.

Does she really think that if you keep denying something, it never happened?

Or is this reality?

Have I been wrong about connecting with the world this

whole time?

"Marta." Steph's voice has sharpened. "Get away from Jeff. You, too, Sonia. I want you both in my office now."

Jenna is crying. I understand how terrible this must be for her.

Marta is her cousin. Of course she'll be loyal to Marta.

Not to me.

Inside the office, Steph slams the door and stands behind her desk. She does not invite Marta or me to sit down.

I've never seen Steph so angry before.

"All right." Steph points at me. "I want you, Sonia, to say what you saw Marta doing that upset Jeff so much."

I describe the pinching and the scratching and the terror on Jeff's face.

"She's lying," Marta says calmly. "We all know she's a liar."

Is this true?

Is this how everyone thinks of me here at the Center?

Sonia the liar?

"And why would Sonia lie about this, Marta?"

"She wants to get me in trouble because I've worked here the longest and all the children like me the best!"

I feel as if Marta's punching me in the stomach. Her voice is so loud, everyone outside must know what's going on in here by now.

And none of it makes any sense.

"Lower your voice, Marta." Steph's voice is cold. "It'll be your turn to talk in a moment."

Marta glares at me.

"Are you sure about this, Sonia?" Steph doesn't sound or

look particularly friendly.

"Yes," I say. "I know what I saw."

In my head, my usual demons of doubt and indecision try to get me to take the words back. Because I want so badly for the Center to be the way it was before.

But I know nothing will ever be the same.

And I am not doing this for me. I am doing it for Jeff.

Exactly the way I would want someone to do it for Sara.

Except Sara will never need anyone else to stand up for her. She has Peter and Alessia, for God's sake.

And me.

"All right, Marta. It's your turn to speak now." Steph looks at her.

But Marta crosses her arms over her chest and shakes her head. "You're both nurses," she says. "It's nurses against aides. No one is going to believe me."

Steph's shoulders sag. "That's absolutely not true, Marta. We will conduct a thorough investigation."

Steph's voice is shaking because it's clear that Marta has no faith in what she's saying.

"You've worked here for a long time, Marta," Steph insists. "You've earned your place at the Center. No one has ever had a problem with you."

Marta points to me. "Then why don't you have a problem with Sonia lying about me?"

"Start by telling me what happened," Steph says reasonably.

"I was doing Jeff's physical therapy," Marta says, her face sullen. "Then, all of a sudden, *she*—(pointing at me)—rushes over and starts screaming. She's crazy! Everyone knows that. I wasn't doing anything."

Steph looks at me.

"Sonia, do you have any proof that Marta was hurting Jeff?"

No. I don't.

For the next half hour, Steph keeps asking the same questions, and Marta and I keep giving the same answers.

I'm starting to feel that I made this whole thing up inside my head.

I must be wrong.

After all, I've made so many mistakes. And been wrong about so many things in my life.

I don't want to mess up someone else's life if there's any chance this is my mistake

In fact, maybe this is all my fault.

Maybe that's just the way my life is.

And always will be.

My own fault.

Except I know what I saw.

And finally, I realize there's someone else who knows it, too.

"Steph," I say, "you should ask Louise."

"*What?*" Steph looks disgusted.

"We're not getting a child involved in a staff dispute, Sonia. How could you even suggest such a thing?"

Marta sneers at me.

"But Steph, Louise saw it too. And she may have seen it before."

I describe how Louise pinched me in the butt and pushed me around with her wheelchair until I saw what Marta was doing.

"She's lying about that, too!" Marta says.

Her eyes bore into me as if this denial alone will get me to change my story.

"Louise hates her. Everyone knows that."

I can't say that Louise is one of my favorite people. But I didn't know the aides were keeping tabs on how I treat the children.

"Fine."

Steph's voice is like an icicle scraping against a mailbox.

"If there was nothing to see, Louise will have nothing to contribute. But we're asking her now."

She opens the door of her office and motions both of us to go out in front of her.

Outside, all the aides pretend to be absorbed in their own business with the children. No one looks at Steph, Marta, or me.

Especially not Jenna.

I was right. They heard everything.

They must all hate me now.

Steph goes over to Louise's wheelchair. She sits down close to her and turns Louise's head, so Louise is looking at Steph's hands.

Then she signs.

Louise only responds to the nurses who are most important at the Center. She knows that Steph is the head nurse.

So, she signs back.

And Steph's face goes blank with shock.

She turns around and looks at the two of us.

"In my office, *now*."

Behind closed doors, I put my hands behind my back so no one can see how badly they are shaking.

"I asked Louise if she knows who has been hurting Jeff," Steph says. "Louise says it's you, Marta."

Chapter Thirty-Three

You could not get at Mary, either to punish her or to love her; but Maeve did not know that. Her own heart cried out for justice, while there is no justice—only consequences.
–M.J. Farrell (Molly Keane), *Taking Chances*

Steph calls the police. And Marta is taken away.

We are devastated.

Every single one of us.

I feel responsible for all of this.

I've ruined Marta's life.

I've lost Jenna as a friend.

I can't believe this day that started out so well turned out this way.

Never, in a million years, would I have suspected Marta.

She's worked here so long. What happened?

If Marta can become a monster who hurts a child, what does that say about me?

Or Steph? Or anyone?

"I know Marta's been very upset for a while now," Steph tells me. "Her son overdosed last year. He's in rehab but he's not doing well."

Why didn't I know this?

Would it have made any difference if I knew and talked to Marta?

Why didn't I help her? Connect with her?

I can't believe that I was in danger of disconnecting from my own family only months ago.

Was I that careless? Uncaring?

I could have become Marta.

It's only because of Peter that I didn't.

When I get home on Sunday night, I will make it up to him.

I will love him. Even when he irritates me.

I will pay more attention to Alessia. Even if that means I have to ask her if she wants to go home to Italy.

I will make sure that every minute I spend with Sara, I am there for her.

Not thinking about being somewhere else. Not travelling.

I also know that many times, I will mess things up. Maybe I won't be able to fix them all.

Terrible things will happen. The way they did to Marta.

And to my friend who was raped.

On some days, Sara will be sick. Or angry at me.

I will get annoyed with Peter. I always do.

On some Fridays, my train will be canceled so I will miss work. Or I won't be able to get home on time on Sunday night.

Peter will get mad when this happens, and he will want me to quit work.

When life is stressful for me, when things don't go the way, I think they should, I will want to run away.

Maybe, some days, I will.

But now I know I will come back.

Wait.

I'm doing it again.

I'm thinking about the future instead of being here taking care of what's in front of me right now.

Right now, there is something I can do.

For someone I have always ignored.

I take my med cart back to Louise.

As usual, she won't look at me.

I take all the special treats off my cart and put them in her lap.

"Thank you, Louise," I say.

She turns her wheelchair away.

The treats are not enough.

Tomorrow, I'll order Louise the special American Girl doll that we all know she wants. The one she points to when the catalog arrives. With all the overpriced outfits.

It's a Disney princess doll, and a complete waste of money, but I will pay for it myself. Gladly.

And, from now on, I will treat Louise like a princess.

The way I treat Gulie.

And Thomas.

And Jeff.

And the other children.

Because if I didn't realize before that we are all connected, I do now.

We are all travellers.

Acknowledgments

When I wrote this book, I asked a group of friends and some fellow writers to provide input. Sincere thanks to Lorna Lally, Hilary Lally (Lorna Lally's incredible mom), Richard Price, Lee Lichtenstein, Allen Frances, Kathy Wojtas, and Jennifer Betancourt for reading and critiquing this manuscript at an earlier stage. Your comments were extremely helpful. Also, I want to thank Gavi, Inga, David, and Nathan for putting up with me while I wrote this book chapter by chapter. Finally, thanks to the world's best grandchildren: Bella, Nia, River, Ani, and Nele. Everything I write is for you.

About the Author

Lin Betancourt is a writer employed as a grandmother. She has written several children's books and one other book for adults. She enjoys reading, baking, and finding arcane museums to visit.